"So what k... ...want to play?"

Carter watched Nikki shuffle the cards and continued, "Five-card stud? Seven-card draw?"

"Strip." Nikki's smile bordered on a leer. She'd never played strip poker before. Suggesting it was very naughty of her, but she'd had it. Actually, she *hadn't* had it, she just wanted it. Carter had been devouring her with his eyes for the past hour, and she wanted to call his bluff, so to speak.

"Very funny," Carter said without laughing. "Now, where are the chips?"

"Don't have any. That's why I think strip poker is such a good idea."

"It's not a good idea."

Carter's reluctance excited her. She was beginning to enjoy being a wicked woman. This was a facet of her personality that even *she* hadn't known about. She wished she were wearing less clothes. But that could be arranged—if she played her cards right.

Heather MacAllister lives in Houston, Texas, with her electrical-engineer husband and her two live-wire sons. A former music teacher who traded a piano keyboard for a computer keyboard, she enjoys researching her books and is not above involving her family. The boys suggest future stories revolve around food, video games and extended school holidays. Heather threatens to write one about sons who do all the cooking and housework.

Heather's fans will be happy to know that she is already working on a sequel to *Jilt Trip*. Watch for *Bedded Bliss*, Dee-Ann and Julian's story, coming to Temptation early in 1996.

Books by Heather MacAllister

HARLEQUIN ROMANCE
(writing as Heather Allison)

JILT TRIP
Heather MacAllister

Harlequin Books

TORONTO • NEW YORK • LONDON
AMSTERDAM • PARIS • SYDNEY • HAMBURG
STOCKHOLM • ATHENS • TOKYO • MILAN
MADRID • WARSAW • BUDAPEST • AUCKLAND

To Sharon Wright, my first fan

Many thanks to those of you who encouraged me as I wrote
this book, including, but not limited to—in case I leave
someone out—Pat, Alaina, Marilyn, Sue, Carla, Christina,
Barb, Betty, Susan W., Susan Mac, Anne, Jan, Bonnie,
Marian, Vicki, Vikki, Laurel, Elaine, Carolyn, Day, Arnette,
Janice, Susie, Marie, Jane, Anna, Jodi, Karen, MJ, Hollis,
Sandy, Thelma, Roz, Christie, Harriet, Allison and Laura.

ISBN 0-373-25643-4

JILT TRIP

Copyright © 1995 by Heather W. MacAllister.

1

THE ORGAN PLAYED softly. Gardenias scented the air. The sunlight of a warm Galveston June day filtered through the stained-glass windows. Bridesmaids gathered in the vestibule of the church. Guests murmured in anticipation.

And the groom's pager beeped. Again.

"Damn!" Carter Belden slapped the button in annoyance, then remembered the somber presence of the Reverend Royer waiting to lead him toward the altar. "I beg your pardon."

Reverend Royer's eyebrows knit together. "Perhaps you could, er, turn off the sound for the duration of the ceremony?"

"Of course," Carter murmured. Glancing at the number on the pager's display, he exhaled. "It's my office. I'll have to call in."

"Mr. Belden!"

"My best man isn't here yet," he reminded the openmouthed minister. "This could be from him."

Reverend Royer shook back the sleeve of his robe and checked his watch. "He'd better hurry or he'll miss the ceremony!"

"We've got a few more minutes, don't we?"

"Y-yes, but—"

"Stall, if you have to." Carter was already striding through the groom's anteroom toward the church's administration area.

Robe flapping, Reverend Royer hurried after him. "But what shall I tell the bride?"

His hand on the doorknob, Carter paused. "Tell Dee Ann it's business. She'll understand."

Dee Ann might understand, but Carter didn't. He'd always known he had a loyal and dedicated staff of fellow workaholics, but did they really expect him to conduct business moments before he took his place at the altar?

This had to be an emergency, but that's what he'd thought the four other times they'd paged him this morning. He knew they weren't thrilled about his marriage to the daughter of a business competitor, but they should come to the wedding anyway, damn it.

Saunders, at least, should be here. He was Carter's lawyer, good friend and supposedly the best man.

Where *was* he?

Probably trying to persuade Nikki Morrison to come.

Slowing his pace, Carter visualized his petite dynamo of a comptroller, with her green eyes and the freckles that showed no matter how she tried to cover them up.

Ah, Nikki . . . Carter smiled. Well, maybe he could understand if Nikki didn't want to come, though she'd seemed to accept his approaching nuptials with her usual calm professionalism.

Closing the glass door to the church reception area, Carter reached for the phone on the desk and quickly punched out the number. Through the intercom system, he could hear the organ music. It didn't sound like the bridal march yet.

"Carter?"

It was Nikki's voice, tense and breathless.

His collar suddenly felt tight. "What's going on, Nikki? Where's Saunders?"

"Are we too late?"

Carter exhaled through his teeth. "In three minutes, I'm supposed to be standing at the altar *with* Saunders. Where in the *hell* is he?" He winced and looked around to see if anyone had overheard. A painting of an unknown saint stared at him reprovingly. Carter turned his back.

"Carter?" A different voice.

"Saunders? Where in the . . . world are you?"

"We're in the car." The lawyer sounded weary. "Don't start without us." His chuckle fell flat.

At least Saunders hadn't been in an accident. Yet. "It would serve you right if you *did* miss my wedding."

"*No!*"

The chorus of no's startled him. "Are Julian and Bob in the car with you?"

"Yes." Nikki's voice came through the wires again.

"But I saw Bob's wife and kids here." *What* was going on?

"Carter, wait for us. You've got to listen to what we've found."

"This isn't about your takeover—"

"Shh! We're on the cellular."

Carter clamped together his lips in frustration. Cellular phone conversations could be overheard by anyone with a radio and they all knew not to discuss business on one. It wasn't like him to forget.

"Just wait until we get there," Nikki pleaded. "I've got to talk with you before you marry Dee Ann."

"She's right," Saunders broke in. "Don't do anything before hearing us out."

"This is unbelievable."

Behind him, he heard a tapping sound on the glass windows. Turning, Carter saw Reverend Royer and Miss Hicks, the wedding coordinator. Both wore identical expressions of alarmed urgency.

Carter shrugged and pointed to the telephone. Miss Hicks opened the door. "Mr. Belden, we're behind schedule."

"Just a moment," he murmured into the receiver. Mustering a soothing smile, Carter said to the coordinator, "Tell everyone I'll pay for overtime."

"Money isn't the point, Mr. Belden. Time is."

The corners of Carter's smile drooped cynically. In his experience, money was usually the point. "Have the photographer take some more pictures of the blushing bride." Dee Ann liked being photographed.

"He's videotaping in the balcony."

"He can't be taping much without me, can he?"

Miss Hicks pursed her lips.

Carter tried another smile. "My best man is running late."

"There are two weddings scheduled this afternoon after yours," Reverend Royer informed him. "It *is* June, you know."

"If you run late, *they'll* run late," Miss Hicks added.

Carter would have offered to pay for their overtime, as well, but he knew it wouldn't matter. "Do you hear this, Nikki?" he asked into the phone.

"Tell them to start without you."

"Very funny."

"You're doing a great job of stalling," she said. "We're just a few blocks away."

"I'm hanging up the telephone now, Nikki. I'm turning off my pager. You've got ten minutes. No more." He hung up the telephone.

"Ten minutes?" He smiled at the minister and the wedding consultant, who both looked at their watches, then at each other. They were starting to get on his nerves. It was *his* wedding, too. What were they going to do, hold the ceremony without him?

"I'll inform the organist and Miss Karrenbrock." Miss Hicks hurried into the bowels of the church.

Carter turned off his pager. Instantly, it beeped.

As he stared at it, Reverend Royer reached beneath his robe and smiled apologetically. "Mine this time, I'm afraid. As long as we're waiting...?" He gestured toward the telephone and Carter stepped out of the way.

Shoving his hands into the pockets of his gray morning suit, Carter strolled back to the groom's anteroom.

Dee Ann would be furious, though she'd never show it. A cool blond Texas belle, Dee Ann understood perfectly the relationship between men, business and the money to pay for designer clothes and personal trainers. It had been bred into her. The epitome of a corporate wife, she would never interfere in his business affairs.

But that didn't mean she wouldn't expect compensation for her tolerance.

Carter didn't mind. It amused him to watch her try to manipulate him and to allow her small victories now and then.

He could afford them.

Marrying Dee Ann was the best idea he'd had in a long time. She would make a fabulous wife and that's what he wanted: an old-fashioned arrangement where she managed home and hearth, and he concentrated on making the money to pay for it. Although he enthusiastically supported women's rights, he also recognized that he couldn't be the type of husband a career woman needed.

He'd tried it once already with disastrous results. With both partners concentrating on their careers, nobody concentrated on the marriage.

Carter wasn't going to make *that* mistake again.

It wasn't fair to ask a woman to give up her career, but Dee Ann made no secret that she considered marriage and community service a career. Carter admired her for her honesty. He also knew that they wouldn't need a second income like many families. Dee Ann would find fulfillment in her work on the boards of various charities, and he was willing to support her endeavors. It was the perfect blending of needs and wants.

Yes, they'd have a good life together.

That is, if Saunders and the others ever got here.

Carter paced in front of the window of the small anteroom and forced himself not to look at his watch. He wanted to sit down, but that would wrinkle his suit. Instead, he checked his appearance in the wall mirror.

His boutonniere was wilting. He had no idea how the rest of him appeared. Of course, if his best man were here, *he* could tell him how he looked, straighten his cravat, make certain his pants cuffs weren't turned up, that sort of thing.

The organist was playing something Carter had heard already. Thank heaven it wasn't the processional.

He patted his pocket, reassured by the lump Dee Ann's wedding ring made. How fortunate he'd decided to hold on to it since clearly Saunders's skills as a best man left much to be desired.

"Carter? You in here?" A flushed Saunders peered inside the room.

"Glad you could make it," Carter drawled, to hide his relief.

"What is this place?" Saunders grimaced as he took in the room and its "furnishings."

"The groom's dressing area," Carter told him with a sweep of his hand.

"They've stuck him back here in the storage room," Saunders called over his shoulder. There were answering voices and then the door fully opened. Saunders entered, followed by Julian and Bob.

And Nikki.

Carter was unaccountably glad to see her. In spite of their turbulent history, they were friends and he valued that friendship—his only one with a woman.

"You had me worried, there." Carter clasped Saunders on the shoulder. Everything would be fine now.

"We have to talk to you," Nikki stated.

Carter nodded. Anything. "Let's get this ceremony over with and I'll slip away during the reception." He pushed Saunders toward the door.

"Now," Nikki ordered just as Saunders dug in his heels.

In surprise, Carter turned and saw that the others all wore grim expressions.

Clutching papers, Nikki walked toward him.

"Use the podium," Saunders suggested, dragging one away from the wall.

"Julian—" Nikki nodded to him as she opened folders "—stand by the door."

"Gotcha." Julian opened it, and checked both directions before closing the door and leaning against it.

"What's going on?" Carter demanded. They were starting to alarm him.

"Stock transactions," Nikki told him.

"Not that again." Carter felt his anger rise. All morning, they'd pestered him with their takeover theories.

"Look." Bob, his chief accountant, adjusted his glasses and pointed to several columns of figures. "This is Belden Industries' stock activity over the past two months compared with this same period last year."

Carter glanced at the figures. "So? That doesn't prove anything." Carter looked at their unsmiling faces. Obviously, he'd have to study those figures at greater length. "Well, there's certainly nothing there so startling that I'd have to postpone my wedding."

"These are the buyers and sellers," Bob continued as if Carter had said nothing.

"Your future father-in-law has bought a sizable chunk." Nikki pointed to the entries under Karrenbrock Ventures.

Carter looked hard at her. "Again, so? I consider that a vote of confidence."

Nikki exchanged a glance with Saunders.

"According to the prenuptial agreement, you promise to transfer ten percent of your holdings in Belden Industries to Dee Ann on condition of your marriage," Saunders said.

He remembered that Saunders and Nikki had howled over that one. "You knew that long ago," Carter said.

Nikki pointed to Bob's figures. "Added to the Karrenbrock holdings, that ten percent would entitle them to a seat on the board of directors."

Carter smiled. "I'm putting the stock in Dee Ann's name. It'll still be in the family."

Nikki's eyes widened and Carter felt a pang of guilt. Stressing Dee Ann's new status was too harsh, he supposed, but they were interrupting his wedding, damn it.

Saunders cleared his throat. "It would be considered Dee Ann's separate property—hers to do with as she pleases."

"And there's nothing to stop her from selling her share to her father," Julian said from his post at the door. "Should he choose to exercise his rights, Karrenbrock would be in a position to seriously weaken Belden Industries."

"That's not going to happen," Carter insisted.

"Or," Nikki said, "her father could give her *his* holdings."

Carter hadn't considered that. "And I bet that's exactly what he's going to do!" he said. "A wedding gift. I've been trying to buy back some Belden stock."

They looked unconvinced.

Carter spread his hands. "Look." He forced a light laugh. His friends' grim faces were more appropriate for a funeral than a wedding. "Dee Ann has no interest in business." He directed his next remarks to Nikki. "She's not like you."

Nikki tilted her chin up. "So I've been told."

Meeting her stare, it occurred to Carter that she wasn't taking his marriage as well as he'd thought.

"Okay. I'll concede that you all have legitimate concerns." Relief flickered across their faces. "Let's go have a wedding and we'll discuss it later."

"It'll be too late then!" Saunders sounded panicked.

Ignoring him, Carter searched the pile of empty drycleaning bags and various wrappings on the ancient sofa, located the best man's boutonniere and removed the plastic. The carnation was still fresh. "Hold this." He handed the flower to Bob, unpinned his own and thrust it at Nikki. "Pin that on Saunders, would you?"

"But . . . you can't still be going through with the wedding after what we've discovered?"

"Careful with that," Carter advised himself as he pinned on the fresh carnation. Saunders should be doing this. Or Nikki.

"There's something else," Nikki added with an edge of desperation in her voice.

When Carter heard it, he felt a surge of pride. Their concern for his company went far beyond that of mere employees. They considered it *their* company, too.

However, he reminded himself abruptly, it wasn't their company and this nonsense had to stop. "Later."

"No!" Nikki gripped his arm on one side, Saunders on the other.

"Hey! You'll wrinkle my jacket."

"Carter." Bob opened more folders. "Karrenbrock Ventures owns Lacefield Foods. Two weeks ago, Lacefield bought stock in Belden Industries."

That caught his attention. "Let me see that." Carter took the folder from his chief accountant and scanned the information. Sighing, he handed it back. "It isn't much."

"Not by itself," Bob admitted. "But I suspect that more of the companies in these files are subsidiaries of Karrenbrock Ventures."

"It's a bad time to be signing away ten percent of your holdings," Julian said.

Carter studied the faces of his trusted employees and friends. Julian, his executive vice president, the unflappable connoisseur of art and women. Bob, the balding accountant. The always-anxious Saunders, and Nikki . . .

She held her body stiffly and had a death grip on the files. There was something in her expression that went beyond concern for the welfare of Belden Industries. Carter stared at her the longest, compelled by the intensity of her gaze and the . . . panic? That didn't make sense. It was as if she was *willing* him to postpone his wedding.

A smile of regret pulled at his lips. *Our time has come and gone, kid.* If they'd been alone, he would have said it aloud.

Addressing the group, he asked, "So, on the basis of one company's buying an insignificant amount of stock, you want me to call off my wedding?"

Everyone looked at one another. Nikki spoke.

"Just postpone it until we can determine exactly how much stock Karrenbrock controls and through what companies."

"You've got to be kidding."

She shook her head. "He'll make his move on Monday, while you're on your honeymoon. By the time you figure out what's happened, it'll be too late to counter."

"That's absurd." But he could tell the others agreed with her.

"No, it's perfect," she persisted. "Who'd suspect it?"

"He's going to be my *father-in-law!*" Carter stared at them. Obviously, Nikki had managed to convince everyone to see things her way. "It doesn't make sense. Why would he do that to me?"

Julian shrugged. "Probably because he can."

"Karrenbrock is ruthless, but humiliate his daughter's husband?" Carter shook his head. "Dee Ann would never forgive him."

"She's probably in on it," Nikki retorted.

Carter felt like ripping their papers apart. Instead, he gripped the edge of the podium. "You're angry because I'm giving her ten percent, aren't you?"

"You're still vulnerable, even without giving Dee Ann ten percent," she replied.

"I *did* advise against selling stock to finance that oil drilling project," Bob piped up in an I-told-you-so tone.

"And I relayed your concerns to Carter," Nikki assured him, "along with my own."

Bob addressed Carter. "Perhaps she didn't *emphasize*—"

Carter glared him back into silence.

"The minister's coming," Julian said seconds before Reverend Royer sailed into the room.

"Mr. Belden . . . and best man?"

"Here!" Saunders stepped forward, holding the battered carnation.

"Saunders!" Nikki hissed.

"Let's go." Carter moved forward.

"*Carter!*" Nikki shrieked.

Everyone froze.

Nikki had gone white, and her freckles stood out like the cinnamon on Carter's morning cappuccino. She *hadn't* accepted that he was marrying Dee Ann. His heart twisted for her.

"Could we have a few more minutes?" he asked the minister.

"Young man." Reverend Royer inhaled deeply. "Miss Karrenbrock is waiting in the vestibule with her bridesmaids. The organist has repeated "Sheep May Safely Graze" no less than five times. Miss Hicks is bemoaning a melting ice sculpture and the candles are beginning to drip. May I suggest you conduct your business at a later time?"

Carter gritted his teeth. "Why don't you start without me, then?" He heard a strangled sound from Nikki's direction and didn't dare look at her.

"I'll be praying for you in the antechamber." Reverend Royer piously withdrew.

"Now look what you've done!" Carter rounded on Nikki. "I've insulted a man of God!"

"Nikki," Saunders began, "just tell—"

She held up her hand. "If—if you're determined to go through with this marriage—"

"I am."

"Then I'd like to propose a toast," she announced. Julian handed her a bottle of champagne. The cork had already been popped.

"You have all lost your minds," Carter said in amazement.

Saunders solemnly produced paper cups and handed him one.

"You can't seriously think I'd greet my bride with alcohol on my breath!" No one met his eyes. "It's not even a good vintage."

"Well, she didn't want to ruin—*ow!*" Julian broke off.

"Sorry." Nikki, the bottle shaking slightly, poured a little champagne into each cup. When she reached Carter, she filled his to the brim.

"So is this your new plan?" He tapped the cup. "Get me drunk and I won't go through with the wedding?"

Everyone stared at his own cup.

They were so transparent, Carter thought. "You'd like that, wouldn't you?" Gazing at them defiantly, Carter held his cup aloft. "To Dee Ann Karrenbrock, may she prove you all wrong." He drained his cup in a single gulp. The domestic champagne tasted even worse than he'd expected. It wasn't like Julian to select something so inferior.

Didn't Julian, one of his best friends, think Carter's bride was worth a toast with the finest champagne?

Lowering the cup, Carter was immediately aware that no one had drunk with him. His face heated with anger at the insult.

His eyes narrowed. "Aren't you going to propose a toast to my happiness, N-Nikki?" His tongue stuck to the roof of his mouth. Nasty vile stuff. He thrust out his cup, anyway.

Nikki clutched the bottle so tightly, her knuckles were white.

"More," he commanded.

Nikki filled his cup.

No one said anything.

"I'm waiting."

"May you find happiness in spite of yourself," she said, her eyes mocking him as he quaffed his drink.

The second cup went straight to his head. Carter clutched the podium as the room wobbled. Damn cheap champagne.

"Carter?" Two Nikkis spoke to him. He closed his eyes. One Nikki was more than enough.

"'S hot." He tried to loosen his collar, but the pearl stickpin got in the way.

Saunders took his arm. "Do you want to sit down?"

Irritated, Carter shook off his lawyer's hand. "Wrinkle my panths." Oh, great. His tongue was swollen. How could he recite his vows? Maybe if he practiced.

"I, Cawtuh, take thee, Dee Ann, do be mah lawfoolly weddud wahf..."

"What's he saying?"

"Shh."

Water. He needed water. Cold water would shrink his tongue and cool his burning face. He took a step backward and the room tilted, then began a slow spin.

Drunk?

Dee Ann would be livid.

"Not dunk," he muttered. Not on two paper cups of champagne.

"Carter, sit down." Saunders urged him in the other direction.

"No." He closed his eyes against the spinning room and concentrated on putting one foot directly in front of the other. He would stand in front of that altar. He *would* marry Dee Ann...

"Carter! Carter... Car-ter... Caaaaar-terrrr..."

The sound came from all around him. He took another step and missed the floor.

Clawing at air, he landed on his knee, then fell prone.

His boutonniere would be completely crushed. Trying to save it, he rolled over and opened his eyes. Four anxious faces peered down at him. Four anxious and guilty faces.

He was the only one on the floor.

Black ringed his vision as the faces receded down a tunnel.

Realization struck. "Dug! You... dug me." He tried to point, but his arm was too heavy to lift.

A cool hand touched his forehead. Huge green eyes filled his vision. From a distance, he heard, "Trust me."

Through sheer force of will, Carter managed a reply as darkness overtook him. "Fahd! Yoo awl fahd!"

2

"FIRED? *Fired?* I heard him say fired." Saunders shredded what was left of the carnation. "He fired us, didn't he?"

Nikki sat back on her heels. "Sure sounded like it."

"Oh, no, oh, no," Bob, the chief accountant, groaned. "I'm refinancing my mortgage. I can't refinance if I'm out of work. And I've got to lock in my rates!" He grabbed Julian's arm. "This might cost me as much as one and a half percentage points!"

Julian clamped a hand on the accountant's shoulder. "Carter's drunk. The man can't make valid business decisions when he's drunk."

"You know he's not drunk!" Bob said in disbelief.

"I don't know anything of the kind." Julian, his hand still on Bob's shoulder, hustled him toward the door.

Bob's eyes bulged. "But . . . but—"

"It isn't uncommon for a groom to take something to calm his nerves," Julian stated, calmly brushing away the wrinkles Bob had left on the arm of his perfectly cut suit. "He probably shouldn't have had alcohol with it, though."

"But—"

"Bob." Nikki cut him off. She signaled Julian with a jerk of her head.

He opened the door. "Did you actually *see* anything unusual prior to Carter's drinking the champagne, Bob?"

"No, but—"

"Neither did we," Julian said as they left the room.

"Remind me not to involve Bob in any more high-level management decisions," Nikki muttered.

"They're coming back, aren't they?" Saunders began to hyperventilate.

She eyed him with dismay. "Not you, too?"

Saunders threw away the remnants of his boutonniere. "Why couldn't you have just *told* him?"

Nikki looked down at Carter and brushed a strand of hazel hair off his forehead. She knew his eyes, if they were open, would match. She'd always thought it an extremely attractive combination.

"Nikki?" Saunders squatted beside her.

She sighed. "He wouldn't have believed me."

"I would have backed you up."

"You're backing me up now," she said ruefully. "Besides, I didn't want anyone else to know."

"You mean...you mean, even *Julian* doesn't know?"

Nikki shook her head.

"How did you talk him into this?"

"With Julian, it's all a matter of approach. I believe he was dating Dee Ann and introduced her to Carter. She immediately dropped Julian and went on to bigger game."

"And now he's getting even. I thought he bought into our takeover theory too fast."

Nikki reached out and gripped Saunders's hand. "It'll be okay. Carter will be mad, but I know if you keep digging, you'll find that Karrenbrock is planning a takeover, outrageous as it sounds."

Saunders nodded miserably. "How long do you think he'll be out?"

"I have no idea." Nikki eyed Carter, half afraid he'd come to. "They were *your* sleeping pills."

Moaning, Saunders held his head in his hands. A lock of hair slipped, revealing a bald spot. "He'll have us arrested."

"He'll give us a bonus."

"I'll be disbarred."

"You'll receive an official commendation."

"He won't let me be best man."

Nikki glared at Saunders' hangdog face. "Do you *really* think he'll marry Dee Ann after this? Even when...everything's clear?" She refused to consider it. As far as Nikki was concerned, this engagement was kaput. Eventually, perhaps within the next decade, Carter would thank them all.

She loosened Carter's collar and felt his pulse. Slow and steady. Strong. His breathing was fine. He probably wouldn't be out too long.

A single knock sounded at the door. Julian pushed a wheelchair inside and quickly glanced up and down the hallway. "No sign of the good reverend."

"Where's Bob?" Nikki caught the rose-decorated afghan Julian tossed to her.

"In the car."

"He's not going to drive, is he?" she asked.

"Hardly. He's asking for the champagne." Julian inhaled deeply. "I just may give it to him."

"Which reminds me." Nikki got to her feet and gathered the paper cups and bottle, emptying the contents in the nearest potted greenery. "This will liven up their drab lives."

"Uh, Nikki?" Saunders pointed to a growing puddle. "That's a fake plant."

"At least she can't kill it," Julian said.

"Don't say that word!" Saunders pleaded.

"Will you two please get Carter in the wheelchair!" Nikki closed her eyes and reined in her temper. Criminal masterminds they were not. "Everything is going to be fine."

"I'll find something to clean up the mess," Saunders offered, carefully avoiding Carter's comatose form.

Ultimately, it took Nikki's help to maneuver Carter's heavy, limp body into the wheelchair.

"Julian, see if there's a back way out." Nikki arranged the afghan around Carter, concealing everything but his shoes. Then she tied a scarf around his head, Russian peasant style.

"What do you think?" She pulled a few tendrils over his forehead and stepped back.

Saunders looked doubtful. Well, it was too late to quit now.

A tight-faced Julian returned. "There's a back exit, but it would mean wheeling him around on the sidewalk."

"Better than wheeling him through the front of the church," Nikki decided. "Is the coast clear?"

"I'm just about finished here." Saunders swiped at the puddle with something Nikki thought looked horribly like a child's choir robe.

"You *are* finished."

Saunders dropped the white cloth as though it had burnt him.

It was eerily quiet, with nothing but the occasional squeak of the wheels accompanying them as they maneuvered Carter down the hall. About the time Nikki pinpointed what was different, the organ began playing again.

The majestic sound reverberated in the empty halls.

Nikki gasped. "It's 'Trumpet Voluntary'!"

"So?" Julian said over his shoulder.

"That's usually the processional music!" Nikki stopped and listened.

"Hurry up!" Saunders urged, his voice cracking. The pressure was obviously getting to him.

"I don't like the sound of this," she said to Julian. The music continued. "You go on ahead."

"*What?*" Saunders screeched as Julian pulled him along. "She can't abandon us!"

Nikki ignored him and ran in the other direction. She passed by the groom's dressing room and reached the antechamber in time to see Reverend Royer swish through the paneled door.

Good. Maybe he'd stop the organist.

She waited several seconds, breathing quickly.

The music swelled.

Nikki made her way down the dark labyrinthine hallway toward a stream of light seeping from under a door. The music grew fainter. Holding her breath, she stopped in front of the door and slowly cracked it open, hoping it wasn't the sanctuary.

No noise came from inside the room. Nikki pushed the door open farther. She had an impression of peach and blue, with a large mirror surrounded by lights. The scent of perfume and hair spray hung in the air. Plastic clothes bags, tissue paper and other wedding residue littered the sofa.

This was the bride's room.

And it was empty.

"Oh, my God!" she whispered. "They *are* starting without him!"

Hurling herself toward the door across the room, Nikki yanked it open and found herself in the church vestibule.

As she stared, one taffeta-clad bridesmaid began the hesitation step.

Left standing at the entrance was the maid of honor.

And the bride on the arm of her father.

An icy, regal beauty, Dee Ann looked lovely. Her blond hair was upswept and her dress was a stark column of beaded satin. A cathedral train swirled behind her.

Nikki almost felt sorry for her. Dee Ann had obviously decided that the sound of the wedding music would bring Carter to the altar.

How could Nikki stop this? What could she say? For one hysterical moment, she thought about blurting out the truth, but no one would believe her.

Frankly, she found it hard to believe herself.

A small woman dressed in black fussed with the bride's train. No doubt the wedding coordinator or her assistant.

Nikki hissed and beckoned, but the woman ignored her. Creeping forward, Nikki tried again. "I have to talk with you!"

The wedding coordinator, her mouth set in a reproving O flitted toward her. "Shush! We're taping."

The music grew louder and the maid of honor hugged Dee Ann before starting down the aisle.

This was awful. Surely they'd noticed that Carter wasn't there yet?

"You've got to stop her!" Nikki implored the woman.

"I'll do no such thing!"

Nikki lunged toward Dee Ann.

The woman, surprisingly strong for her size, restrained her.

The organ swelled and Dee Ann stepped over the threshold as Nikki watched in horror. "No! The groom isn't there!"

"What are you, hon, an ex-girlfriend?"

Ex. If only she were. "I—he . . . he's sick."

"What do you mean, sick?"

"He suddenly collapsed and...appendicitis, I think."

The woman's fingers dug into Nikki's arms and her face whitened.

"Tell Dee Ann not to worry." Nikki pried the coordinator's fingers off her arm. "We've taken him to get medical attention. But . . ." Trailing off, Nikki pointed to the empty doorway.

With a screech, the woman whirled through it.

Nikki didn't stay to see the disaster unfold. Running down the gray marble steps of the church, she hurried toward one of the three limousines parked in front.

"Did you stop her in time?" Julian asked and opened the car door.

Gasping for breath, Nikki shook her head as she climbed in.

"Oh, boy." Opposite her, a sweating Saunders supported a still-unconscious Carter.

"Oh, boy?" Bob's voice cracked from the front seat. "That's all you have to say? After . . . after . . ." He buried his head on his knees.

Julian slammed the driver's-side door and put the car in gear. Nikki swiveled toward him and placed a restraining hand on his shoulder. "Is Bob up to this?" she asked in a low voice.

Julian shrugged.

With raised eyebrows, Nikki nodded to a quiet Saunders. Shaking his head, Julian rolled his eyes.

Bob moaned.

Nikki reached a decision she hoped she wouldn't regret. "Bob, why don't you stay here and go home with your wife and kids. We need someone to tell us what happens."

"Lucky stiff," Saunders muttered.

"Thank you." Bob sounded so pathetically grateful that Nikki regretted involving him. But he'd been the first one to notice something amiss. He deserved the credit.

Not that he wanted credit for everything they'd done today, she supposed, watching as the mild-mannered accountant scrambled out of the car, bumping his head in his haste.

It would be all right. Nikki planned to take sole responsibility, even if she had to lie to protect the others, though she doubted it would come to that.

Carter could be reasonable, she thought, glancing at his sleeping face. And unreasonable, though she'd seen more of that side than the others had.

Bob slammed the door and without looking back, ran toward the church steps.

Nikki relaxed against the plush seat as Julian pulled away from the curb.

"Think he'll crack?" Saunders asked, looking as though he, himself, was considering it.

Nikki shrugged. "Doesn't matter. I won't let him take any blame. He wasn't that involved."

Saunders sighed. "You know, it might not be up to you."

"What do you mean?"

"We've broken some laws here."

Nikki chewed on the inside of her cheek. "Which ones?"

Saunders gaped at her. "Kidnapping comes to mind."

She gestured to the sleeping Carter. "He fell ill and we're seeking medical attention."

Julian snorted. "The real crime is bottling that bilge and calling it champagne."

Saunders threw up his hands in a gesture of frustration and Carter shifted at the movement, his breath fluttering the ends of the scarf.

"I think we can take the scarf off his head now." Nikki tugged on the knot. "Did you have any trouble?" She'd been afraid to ask.

"Nah." Julian signaled a right turn. "We told the other drivers that the old lady snored when she was asleep."

Old lady. Nikki grinned.

Saunders appeared to have calmed down. "Was it really bad back there, Nikki?"

"Yes." She stared out the tinted window, seeing not the lush palms lining the boulevard, or the restored Victorian houses, but Dee Ann standing in the church, waiting to walk down the aisle.

"How . . . how far . . . ?"

Nikki knew what Saunders was trying to ask. There was breathless silence in the car. "She was walking down the aisle before I finally got the coordinator to listen to me. After that, I ran."

"Good call." Julian's eyes met hers in the rearview mirror.

Saunders looked over at her. "What did you say to her?"

What had she told that woman? "That Carter was sick. I might have mentioned appendicitis."

"Appendicitis?" he asked sharply.

Nikki shrugged. "It was the only emergency disease I could think of."

"Hmm."

"That'll let Dee Ann save face at least," Julian commented as he turned onto Seawall Boulevard.

After that, no one said much.

Nikki stared out the car window as mile after mile of Galveston Island rolled past. The bright midday sun reflected off the murky Gulf of Mexico. Drilling rigs speckled the horizon and sea gulls circled the beach, looking for food scraps among the trash.

Against her will, she recalled the countless times she'd made this same drive with Carter to the same destination: their boat, the *Honey Bee*.

The happiest moments of their brief time together had been spent on the *Honey Bee*. They would leave Belden Industries behind, sometimes without warning, without planning. Carter would appear in the door of her office with a look she immediately recognized and she'd turn off her computer, grab her purse and meet him at the elevator.

The *Honey Bee* had no telephone. No fax machine. A radio and portable television, yes, but they didn't watch much TV. Life was slow. Simple.

They were together and it was enough.

She gazed at the man sleeping next to Saunders.

Carter was driven to succeed and his successes were never enough. As soon as he'd conquer one goal, he'd set himself another.

And Nikki had been right there beside him. She'd been fascinated by him, by his single-minded devotion to the business he'd built. The problem, she knew now, was that there had been too much hero worship on her part. After a while, the very qualities which had drawn her to him, pushed her away.

He hadn't changed. She had.

But now, she suspected he'd changed, too. There had been a time when he wouldn't have hesitated to call off a wedding for a lot less evidence than Nikki and the others had gathered. Belden Industries was everything to him and he was everything to it. Without Carter Belden as its head, Belden Industries wouldn't survive.

Carter Belden worked for no man—or woman. If Victor Karrenbrock gained controlling interest, Carter would walk away, but would leave his essence behind.

A shiver prickled her skin. Today, she would have acted exactly the same even without the other... complication Saunders had discovered.

"Which way?" Julian broke into her thoughts.

"Left at the entrance to Dolphin Bay."

Sand dusted the edges of the two-lane road. Rusty mailboxes lined the entrance to the small beach house neighborhood. Street signs were carved into bleached gray wood. Everything looked the same as it always had.

Nikki felt hot, even inside the air-conditioned car. They were overdressed for the beach, and she couldn't wait to climb aboard the *Honey Bee* and slip into her swimsuit.

The road deteriorated the closer to the beach they traveled. Several children dragging neon-bright beach towels stopped to gawk as the black limousine prowled their street.

"Turn on Conch," she said.

Julian wrestled the big car around the corner, the wheels momentarily sinking into the soft sand. With a lurch, the car popped back onto the road. Nikki sighed.

And there it was—the *Honey Bee*, still berthed in the private cove she leased from a beach-house owner who wasn't interested in boating.

Julian pulled the car as close to the dock as he could and stopped.

With the air conditioner no longer running, the interior of the car quickly became like a sauna.

"Now what?" Saunders asked when Nikki made no move to get out.

"I don't know," she answered, at a loss for the first time since the close of business yesterday, suddenly realizing that it was a Saturday in late June. The height of tourist season. And tourists abounded aplenty.

Why hadn't she foreseen this? She'd driven straight into a casual beach-house community in a black limousine. And she was about to have two formally dressed men carry an unconscious groom aboard a boat.

And nobody would notice?

"Nikki?"

"I'm thinking."

Julian turned and faced her. Both men waited.

Why did *she* have to make all the decisions? "Well." She eyed the curious beach goers and made up her mind. "My dear granny from the old country has come to pay a visit." Nikki tied the scarf around Carter's head again.

"Hey, it worked before," she said when Saunders and Julian exchanged a look. "Release the trunk, Julian."

Opening the car door to a blast of heat, Nikki climbed out, wincing as her black patent pumps sank into the dry sand. Removing the folded wheelchair from the trunk, she struggled to pull it apart.

Sand sifted into her shoes. Sweat dampened the silk blouse beneath her black suit. She'd worn black on purpose. Somehow, the occasion had called for it. But now, with the sun blazing on her back, she regretted it.

Besides, they all looked like gangsters.

The wheelchair ready, she tried to push it toward the open door of the limousine. The wheels sank. And this was without Carter's weight. She sighed. Kidnapping Carter had seemed so simple this morning.

Julian leaned an elbow against the car. Saunders fussed with the afghan.

Carter's face turned ruddy and sweat dampened the hair over his forehead.

"This isn't going to work," Julian said in a low voice. "How are we going to get him into the wheelchair with everybody watching?"

"Can't we just slide him in?"

"He's supposed to be an old woman." Saunders joined them at the door. "We have to treat him with respect. We can't haul him around like a side of beef."

Nikki pushed the chair as close to the open door as she could. "I'll block the view from this side. You and Julian get him in as best you can."

Grumbling, they tugged, pulled and slid Carter into the wheelchair. Nikki tried to keep him covered.

The wheels stuck in the sand. They all stared.

Julian sighed and raked a hand through his hair.

Saunders scanned the distant horizon. "What's happened to me? I had a nice life. I had a job that didn't bore me and supported me in the style I desire." He wiped his forehead. "And what do I do? Why, I drug and kidnap my boss, of course. Then I stick him in the sand to roast like a pig at a luau!"

Carter turned his head in the first sign of recovering consciousness. Three soft gasps were carried away on the gentle beach breeze.

"Doomed." Saunders slumped against the car. "We're all doomed."

"Nonsense." Nikki grabbed hold of the wheelchair handles and tugged. "C'mon. The three of us should be able to move this thing."

They managed—barely. Nikki expected to hear police sirens at any moment. As they bumped along the wooden pier, Carter moaned.

They walked faster and pushed him up the ramp onto the *Honey Bee* and out of sight.

Once on board, the men slung Carter onto the berth in the master stateroom and Julian ran back to the limo for supplies.

In the pilothouse, Nikki started the engine and checked to see that the radio worked. She let out a breath in relief. From here on out, it should be smooth sailing—at least for the *Honey Bee*.

"Nikki?" Saunders stuck his head in. "You're going to have to tell him."

She knew. "Let me handle Carter. You work on the legal end."

"All right, then. Speaking as an attorney, I'd advise you not to venture into international waters."

"I've got to sail out far enough so Carter won't jump overboard and try to swim back."

Saunders gave her a stern lawyer-look. Nikki didn't like his stern lawyer-looks. Saunders, surprisingly, made a very intimidating lawyer. It must be something about the contrast in personae.

"We don't know if the Karrenbrocks will call the police," he warned. "We don't know who thought we looked suspicious here at the beach and called the authorities."

Nikki rolled her eyes. "Any rational person would think we looked suspicious."

Julian was back on board. "I stowed everything below. Looks like you're all set."

"The papers?"

"Right here." He tapped a leather briefcase. "We're going to keep digging. You work on Carter."

Nikki shivered.

"I know," Saunders said with a gentle touch to her arm. "Don't worry. Check in at eighteen hundred hours. We'll be standing by."

She nodded, loathe to see them leave. Both men had shed their jackets and she did likewise, peeling the black gabardine off her sweaty blouse.

They checked in on Carter one last time. He had slipped back into a deep motionless sleep.

"Looks like he'll be out a while yet," Julian said. "At least long enough for you to get away from shore."

Nikki drew a deep breath and nodded.

Julian grinned. "Well, then. Bon voyage."

She watched as he and Saunders walked down the ramp, jackets slung over their shoulders. They reached the bottom, cast off the ropes and waved.

Nikki waved back, then shoved the throttle into reverse.

The *Honey Bee* drifted away from the dock and for the first time in three years, seven months and twenty-two days, Nikki was completely alone with Carter Belden.

Her husband.

3

THE HAPPIEST TIMES of Carter's life were spent aboard the *Honey Bee* with Nikki. Just heading south in the car was enough to loosen the kinks in his shoulders. Inhaling the salty air cleared his mind, the feel of gritty warm sand underneath his feet lowered his blood pressure. As the sun beat on his head, stress evaporated, leaving him pleasantly sleepy.

As soon as the *Honey Bee* was under way, he'd indulge himself in a nap, leaving Nikki at the helm.

Rocked to sleep by the waves of the Gulf of Mexico, Carter always fell into a deep, healing slumber, leaving his well-being in Nikki's capable hands.

He trusted her as he'd trusted no other person. With Nikki, he shared his life and his dreams. When he needed her, she was there for him. Always. Without question.

Ah, Nikki. Just the thought of her filled an emptiness in his life that he hadn't realized was there. He couldn't remember the time before Nikki.

He inhaled with a sigh, reassured by the familiar faint musty smell of the *Honey Bee*'s bedding. Nikki combated mildew with the fervor of a religious zealot, but never completely obliterated it, despite her best efforts.

They so seldom had the opportunity to air the bedding in the master stateroom because it was frequently in use. Once he was in Nikki's arms, he forgot everything but her touch, her scent and her taste. Smiling, Carter burrowed deeper into the pillow.

He supposed they could have adjourned to the guest cabin in the bow on occasion, but it was subject to the movement of the boat more than the master stateroom and not nearly as restful. Not that they rested all that much.

Shifting on the berth, Carter sniffed. Nothing from the galley. Nikki must not have started dinner yet.

He visualized her standing barefoot in the galley, wearing a swimsuit top and cutoff jeans. Her skin would be lightly tanned a peachy bronze, liberally sprinkled with freckles in spite of all the sun block she slathered over her body.

He'd come to depend on Nikki's instantaneous transformation from business partner to domestic goddess. The boat was always stocked. He'd asked her once how she managed to have fresh lettuce, rib-eye steaks and whole milk for his coffee. She told him she always kept provisions in the office refrigerator, rotating them so she and Carter could leave at a moment's notice.

He was grateful, he truly was. He should dictate a memo reminding himself to tell her so. Where was his tape recorder? He tried to search the shelf above the berth, but his arms wouldn't cooperate. They were so heavy...

Lulled by the hum of the generator, Carter drifted back to sleep. Strange dreams disturbed him. Nikki didn't look like Nikki anymore. Her hair was blond instead of chestnut brown. Her eyes were blue instead of ocean green. Her skin was tan and she'd finally managed to get rid of her freckles.

He'd liked her freckles. He'd made several attempts to count them all, but was usually interrupted. An interruption would be welcome now, as a matter of fact. Very welcome.

He waited and the dreams continued, shrouded in swirling white. Nikki in a wedding dress. But Nikki hadn't worn a traditional wedding dress.

Flowers. Nikki had worn mostly flowers. White roses.

Carter smiled, then frowned. Roses were bad, he remembered, but didn't remember why.

In his dreams, he tried to ask the shadowy figures, but no one would tell him. It gave him a headache, though that could have been from the noise. He didn't remember all this humming and pounding on the boat before. Was the beating of his heart sounding in his head?

Maybe if he lay very still, the noise would stop. But stillness was relative, he discovered. Though he didn't move, his body experienced a gentle up-and-down sway. A relentless, never-ending sway.

Carter swallowed, his mouth dry and cottony. He wanted a drink of water, but his stomach immediately rebelled. Hunger...no, seasickness. *Seasick?* Carter Belden was never seasick.

He would will this away. He visualized a grilled rib eye, charred on the outside, bloodred on the inside— and was immediately sorry.

What had happened to his sea legs, or rather his sea stomach? Just how long had it been since he and Nikki had been aboard the *Honey Bee*? Weeks? Months?

Years. The knowledge came to him accompanied by a great sadness. Something had kept him away from the boat. So why was he aboard it now? He cracked open his eyes just enough to see yellow and closed them again. Yes, he was aboard the *Honey Bee*.

But he didn't remember getting to the boat. In fact, the last thing he remembered was . . .

"Nikki!" he bellowed, to his instant regret.

Pain ripped through his head and exploded behind his eyes with such ferocity that he actually opened them to verify that he still had his sight.

He wished he hadn't. The hideous decorating scheme Nikki had chosen for the craft—black, yellow and white stripes—assaulted his vision.

Head throbbing anew, he shut his eyes against the garish yellow walls Nikki thought would add light to the cabins below deck.

He'd indulged her because they were newly married and because the wall covering, yards and yards of it, was fabric, not vinyl. But instead of disintegrating the way he'd expected—and hoped—the heavy canvas had worn like iron.

She'd even had matching swimsuits sewn out of the leftovers, for God's sake. He'd refused to wear his in spite of the hurt looks she'd cast him.

He'd given her a little diamond bee pin to make up for it.

He hadn't seen her wear it in a very long time.

"Carter?" Nikki's voice sounded above him.

"Go away and let me die in peace."

"Hold these."

He felt her take his hand and plop something into his palm. "Does this involve putting anything in my stomach?"

"Aspirin."

"Forget it."

"Carter, having a headache is normal. Aspirin will help."

"Normal? You drugged me."

"Yes."

"There's nothing normal about drugging someone. Therefore, the resulting headache is abnormal."

"Impeccable logic. You're right, as usual," she agreed, cheerfully unrepentant.

"Ha!" He groaned. Being right hurt his head.

"Take the aspirin, Carter."

Moaning piteously, he struggled to sit up. Leaning against the bulkhead, he blindly shoved the pills into his mouth. Nikki practically drowned him with the glass of water. Justice would only be served if he puked all over her, he thought, managing to swallow the pills.

They sloshed around in his stomach as he tried to counter the movement of the boat. "What are we in, a hurricane?" he grumbled.

"No, seas are calm." Nikki maintained that irritatingly serene voice adopted by those who were dealing with grouchy people.

He opened his eyes. The room spun, but he focused on the waistband of her shorts, then tilted his head back and squinted at her.

Kneeling, she tugged away his bow tie and unbuttoned his collar button. She had started on the second button, when he covered her hands with his.

She raised her eyes and he was hit by the force of her green gaze. His pulse drummed in his ears as she awakened feelings long dormant, feelings he thought were dead, not just asleep.

Feelings he had no right to be feeling.

"I'll be right back," she whispered, rocking back on her heels and withdrawing her hands all in one graceful movement. She disappeared out the doorway, returning within moments.

"Don't walk so loud," he mumbled.

Nikki sat on the edge of the berth, doing horrid things to his equilibrium. "Sip some of this. You need lots of liquids."

She wrapped his hands around a warm mug and, only because he knew she'd nag until he cooperated, Carter brought it to his lips.

"Good God almighty, what's this?"

"Defatted chicken broth," she replied in that same conciliatory voice. "It's good for you."

He rolled gritty eyes toward her. "You've shanghaied me. Don't pretend you're concerned about my health."

Her lips drew together in a thin line, her most unattractive expression. "It's your own fault. I had no idea you had become the sort of man who would guzzle champagne moments before he was to walk down the aisle."

"I was provoked. Set up." Since there was nothing else, he drank more broth. Not bad. In fact, the rancid

taste was beginning to leave his mouth. He swallowed
again, noting that he didn't feel as queasy. The stuff
even muffled the drums in his head, allowing a few
thoughts to filter through. "I'm not too clear on recent
events. Am I married?"

Nikki gazed at him steadily. "It's a little complicated, but, yes. You are most definitely married."

"Damn." Carter drained the last of the chicken broth.
"I don't remember the ceremony. I *do* remember passing out," he said sternly. "I don't remember when I came
to. What did I do then, dance on the pews? Insult the
bride's mother?"

Nikki avoided his eyes as she took the mug.

That was a very bad sign. "If I'm married, what am
I doing here? Where's Dee Ann? Is she topside?"

"No."

"Still at the reception?"

"I doubt it."

He tried to visualize Dee Ann in her wedding dress
and couldn't. Another bad sign. "What have you done
to her?"

Nikki glared at him. *"Nothing."*

He folded his arms and focused his eyes until her two
images merged into one. "All right, Nikki. Talk."

Her gaze turned wary, her eyes assessing his mood.

His mood was black, but what did she expect? Fo-
cusing was too much trouble. He closed his eyes. "You
might as well tell me everything."

"I will when you're ready."

He felt her weight leave the berth and grabbed for her
hand, missing but catching her leg instead. "I'm ready
now."

"I'm not," she said, pulling free. "Wait here and I'll be back with the stats."

Stats. And he'd so hoped he wouldn't be required to open his eyes again anytime soon.

While he waited for her return, he peeled off his socks, removed his cummerbund and undid the button Nikki had started to undo, as well as two more.

He was removing his cuff studs by the time she returned.

"All comfy now?" she asked.

Rather than respond, he tossed the studs toward the built-in dresser. One made it, one didn't.

Instead of picking up the stud, Nikki ignored it. "Do you want to look at the papers here, or in the dinette?"

"Here." He watched her carefully as he rolled up his shirtsleeves.

She was doing a good job of maintaining her business persona. Did she find it difficult to do here on the *Honey Bee?* Was she uncomfortable in the master stateroom with him now?

He certainly hoped so.

Sitting down on the berth and tucking one leg underneath her, Nikki spread open a blue file folder across her knee.

Carter's glance swept over it. "This is the same stuff Bob showed me at the wedding."

"But you ignored us at the wedding."

"Obviously a tactical error on my part."

The briefest of smiles flickered across her lips as she pointed to a column of names. "This is a list of major stockholders in Belden Industries. You currently own thirty-eight percent and are still the majority share-holder—"

"Look, Nikki, I don't want to hear all the whys and wherefores right now, just get to the bottom line."

She looked up and said bluntly, "You're going to lose control of your company."

"Impossible," he denied, even as something twisted in his stomach.

Mutely, Nikki gestured to the folder.

She was being an alarmist and he was just seasick. "I don't believe you."

That got to her. "I know you don't," she snapped. "That's why you're here and not on your honeymoon with Miss Texas!"

"That would be *Mrs.* Texas, wouldn't it?"

"Not . . . exactly."

He expected fireworks. Instead, his comment seemed to allow her to regain control and slip back into the I'm-all-business demeanor she'd adopted in the early days after their separation.

He'd hated her cold facade, but understood her reasons. Gradually, excruciatingly, they'd both thawed until, as far as Carter was concerned, everything was back to normal—until he'd announced his engagement to Dee Ann Karrenbrock and Nikki had frozen again. But Nikki wasn't the only one who was cool toward the idea of his marriage to Victor Karrenbrock's daughter.

No one on his staff liked Dee Ann, but then, they didn't have to, did they?

"Nikki, I realize you don't like Dee Ann, so keep her out of this discussion."

"Gladly," Nikki responded.

Carter smiled slightly. "Now," he said, mimicking her tone, "I want information somewhere between that—" he pointed to the blue file "—and losing Belden Industries."

She gazed at him, her mouth set, her eyes narrowing a fraction. "You currently own thirty-eight percent of Belden's stock."

She'd already said that. "*Currently.* I'm buying back more."

"So far, you've been unsuccessful. I own six percent and Julian, Saunders and few others own a combined five percent. That's forty-nine percent."

"Bob's been wringing his hands about that for weeks. What's your point? I realize I'm vulnerable, but it's just under half."

"Just under half if everyone votes your way."

His jaw dropped. "What's—"

"No," she interrupted, shaking her head. "No mutiny in the ranks."

"Then what's the problem?" he demanded, impatient with her. She hadn't told him anything new.

"Upon your marriage, you were going to settle—"

"*Were?*"

"*Carter, will you shut up and listen to me?*"

His head was going to split. "Okay," he whispered.

She lowered her voice. "Ten percent of your stock transfers to Dee Ann. That leaves you with personal holdings of only twenty-eight percent."

Though he had no intention of admitting it to Nikki, Carter hadn't liked the numbers, either, which was why he was so keen on buying back stock. "But I'll still control forty-nine percent."

"Will you?" The words hung in the silence.

Apparently, he'd misjudged her loyalty to him. "What do you own, six percent? Okay, then I'll control forty-three percent. I'm still founder and majority stockholder. People would be foolish to vote against me." Carter found himself unbelievably hurt by her betrayal.

"You pigheaded jerk!" Muttering, Nikki searched through the papers, withdrew one and threw it at him. "See for yourself. Here are all the attempts we made to buy stock compared with actual trades."

Carter snatched the paper and blinked. He hadn't realized how many offers Nikki's department had made. Obviously, he'd have to pay more per share. "It's almost as if someone knew in advance when a block would be available and snatched it right out from under us." Still scanning the columns, he held out his hand. Nikki placed another paper in it.

Although he hadn't spoken, it was exactly the information he'd wanted. Nikki had always been able to anticipate his requests, sometimes even before he'd known what they were. He should concentrate on what she was trying to tell him instead of assuming he was right and she was wrong.

"The buyers are all companies," he commented with a frown.

"We only discovered the connection between Lacefield Foods and Karrenbrock Ventures after the market closed on Thursday. We spent Friday looking for a link with these other companies."

Carter still frowned. "With Lacefield's three percent, that gives Karrenbrock control of seventeen percent. Significant, but not a problem."

Nikki's eyes met his. "With Dee Ann's ten percent, he'd control twenty-seven percent, which nearly equals your personal holdings."

"You're saying my wife would join with her father to vote against me?"

"Either that or join with you and vote against her father."

He'd never thought of it quite that way. He'd known he was vulnerable, but he'd expected to beef up his shares before now. Deep inside, Carter felt the beginnings of panic. He suddenly realized that not since its inception had Belden Industries been at such risk. The paper in his hands quivered and he dropped it on the yellow-and-black-striped spread, disgusted by this outward sign of agitation.

Panic is a response that results from a perceived loss of control, he told himself. Carter was in control. He took a deep breath. He'd remain in control. He'd use the panic to provide an edge, an edge that had been dulled by endless wedding preparations.

"Of course, Saunders, Julian and I will vote our shares with you, which will guarantee you thirty-nine percent without Dee Ann's stock," Nikki assured him. "What concerns us is the possibility that Karrenbrock, through his subsidiaries, controls even more Belden stock."

A legitimate concern, and one he planned to address. "But you don't know for certain."

"We need time to find out."

Carter gazed at her as she returned the papers to the folder, closed it and opened another one.

Mentally, he stepped back to assess the situation and the personalities involved. How much of what Nikki had told him was a valid business concern and how much was fueled by jealousy?

He couldn't blindly accept the fact that his future father-in-law would threaten his company. It made more sense that the man would take steps to strengthen it so that his daughter—and future grandchildren—would benefit. "Why should I be concerned if my father-in-law owns a large chunk of my company? Shouldn't I consider that a show of support?"

"I wouldn't presume to tell you what to consider it, Carter," she responded in a bored voice. "Victor Karrenbrock is a direct competitor in several areas of industrial manufacturing. You recently positioned yourself to enter oil-field supply, one of his main sources of revenue. It's a tight, lean field. He's bound to resent it."

"Business is business," Carter stated reflexively.

"Exactly." Nikki opened another file. "Which is why we suspected that he'd attempt a hostile takeover while you were on your honeymoon."

Preposterous. "And so you took it upon yourself to see that there was no honeymoon." Outrageous.

"We thought it best." She smiled. It was a little smile full of self-satisfaction. It infuriated him.

"You went too far!" Carter swept all Nikki's facts and figures to the floor of the cabin. "You *suspect!*" His voice rose. "*Suspect? Think? Probably?*" He was shouting even though it renewed the pounding in his head. "On such a flimsy premise, you ruined my wedding?"

Nikki, her eyes wide, backed off the berth. "We need more time to verify—"

"Turn this boat around and take me back to my wife!" He groaned and grabbed his temple.

When he released his breath, he distinctly heard her say, "No."

"What do you mean no? I'm ordering you to sail back to the dock."

She laughed. *Laughed.* "On whose authority?"

Was he still asleep? Were his dreams turning into nightmares? "On *my* authority!"

"The *Honey Bee* belongs to me now. I'm her captain and I'll decide where she sails."

This was not the Nikki he knew. This was not the Nikki who worked with him. Worked *for* him. Matching her smug smile, he relaxed. "Then, as your boss, I'm ordering you to return me to shore."

"I don't work for you anymore. You fired me." She looked thoughtful. "Come to think of it, you fired all of us. Better not count on that eleven percent voting your way."

The throbbing at the sides of his temples increased. Without this blasted headache, he'd be able to think his way through this mess. "I rescind my firing. Now, take me back."

Lacing her fingers in front of her, she drew a deep breath. "That wouldn't be wise."

"Okay." Inexplicably, Carter's anger seeped away, leaving him feeling like a deflated balloon. "Nikki, what's done is done. Now I've got to make things right with Dee Ann, or she *will* vote against me."

"Carter..." For the first time, Nikki's calm facade cracked. "Any stock she owns, she purchased herself. The ceremony never took place."

"But you said—" He broke off and jerked his left hand up. No wedding ring encircled his finger. Mutely, he stared at her.

Nikki's mouth twisted. "You aren't married to Dee Ann, you're married to me."

4

"TELL ME you're joking."

She shook her head.

As his hand dropped to the bedspread, Carter's face took on all the hues of a color television set gone bad. Gray. Green. Magenta. White.

The gray bothered Nikki the most. It wasn't a healthy color. With the remnants of the sleeping pills still in his system, she was somewhat concerned. Not overly, because Carter hadn't ingested enough of Saunders's pills to depress his system for an extended period of time. But still, she wasn't exactly an expert on this sort of thing.

"Saunders has confirmed this?"

Nikki nodded.

"But I saw the papers."

"Not the right papers. What we have is a divorce in progress." She braced herself, anticipating the return of the magenta color accompanied by yelling, questions and accusations.

But mostly yelling.

Instead, Carter stared at her blankly, closed his eyes and collapsed on the berth.

Great. The thought of being married to her was so repugnant, he'd fainted.

She'd known the news that they were still married would come as a surprise—okay, a shock—but somewhere, deep inside, she'd hoped Carter would be relieved that he wasn't married to Dee Ann.

And if not relieved, Nikki thought peevishly, he could at least pretend he wasn't so horrified. After all, that meant *she* was still married to *him*. Didn't he care about her feelings?

Look at him; anyone would think he'd suffered a fate worse than death. She poked him with her bare toe.

He winced. "Leave me alone."

"Fine." Nikki watched just until Carter's color stabilized. "When you're ready to talk, I'll be in the pilothouse." She fled, leaving her files scattered all over the floor of the cabin.

What had she expected? she asked herself as she climbed into the captain's chair. She checked to see if the autopilot had deviated from the course she'd set when Carter had shouted for her earlier. Straight and true.

Nikki scanned the horizon and the barely visible shoreline. Perhaps she'd sail out another half hour, then anchor. She had no destination in mind other than far enough from shore to prevent Carter from attempting to swim back.

And wasn't *that* a flattering thought. She'd expected too much. She'd underestimated the opposition—Dee Ann and her wiles.

She'd assumed that Carter's number-one priority was still Belden Industries and that all she had to do was point out the threat to get him to act.

Marriage to Dee Ann was a threat. Dee Ann was a threat. She'd cut Carter from the herd as neatly as a Border collie at lambing time. Somehow, Dee Ann had managed to convince Carter that marriage to her would enhance Belden Industries, which Nikki knew from painful personal experience was the only way to manipulate Carter.

That and drugging him.

But it shouldn't have come to that. The Carter she knew would have postponed the wedding on less evidence than they'd collected.

He couldn't . . . surely he didn't *love* Dee Ann?

Nikki felt a twinge of despair, a twinge she ruthlessly smothered. Carter wasn't capable of loving anyone or anything but his company.

When she'd sailed out far enough, Nikki checked her charts to determine the water depth before dropping anchor. Once the line went slack, she put the engine in reverse and slowly let out more line. Judging the angle sufficient, she secured the anchor line to the deck and then backed up the boat until she felt the anchor grip the ocean bottom. By the time Nikki cut the engine and flipped on the drag alarm, it was nearly eighteen hundred hours—six o'clock. Check-in time.

Nikki decided she had enough time to peek in on Carter. She'd expected him to come roaring up on deck at any moment and her nerves were shot.

Descending to the master stateroom brought back vivid memories of past cruises. Countless times, Nikki had prepared their dinner, then awakened Carter from his comalike sleep. Countless times, their dinner had gone cold while they assuaged another hunger.

Wending her way through the dinette and salon, she stopped in the companionway, overcome by the memories of cherished moments from her marriage to Carter.

She'd finally learned to wait to grill the steaks. Carter would emerge from the shower and they'd spend hours entwined with each other, the rhythm of the waves lapping against the boat echoing the rhythms of their lovemaking.

Just then, the *Honey Bee* tilted, punctuating her memories with a tangible reminder and Nikki smiled wistfully.

By the time they'd climbed back on deck, it was usually nighttime. Carter would choose a bottle of wine and Nikki would throw a couple of steaks on the minuscule grill attached to the galley stove. Carter would return and carry their bowls of salad topside and Nikki would follow with the steaks, charred on the outside, red in the middle—just the way Carter liked them.

Under a canopy of stars, they'd talk and eat and watch the passing ships with their running lights and admire the stark beauty of the oil rigs, twinkling like a forest of Christmas trees growing in the ocean.

In those moments, Carter was hers, all hers. No telephone interruptions. No late business meetings. No paperwork. Just life at its best.

And she'd still managed to lose him.

But then, she wondered with a bittersweet ache, had he ever truly been hers?

Gripping the doorway, she peered inside. Carter lay sprawled on his back, his chest rising and falling in a slow, steady rhythm.

He was asleep, just as he'd slept dozens of times before. She stood and watched him, just as she'd stood so many times in the past.

Her bitterness melted away, leaving an aching regret that was dangerously close to self-pity.

Snap out of it. She should call Saunders. Right now. But she couldn't leave the doorway.

Even unconscious, with his mouth slightly open, the soft sounds of his breathing likely to change to snores in a moment, she was drawn to Carter. His white shirt, rumpled now and open at the neck, revealed golden chest hair and her fingers ached to feel the remembered softness of it.

A swell rocked the boat and Carter turned his head, closing his mouth, leaving his lower lip slightly extended. Nikki remembered the feel of that mouth.

She longed to touch him again and this would be her only chance. Giving in, she approached the berth and smoothed his hair away from his forehead. Even that simple platonic action set her heart racing.

His skin was warm, but cooler than before. When he didn't move, Nikki let her knuckles trail over his jaw and down the side of his neck.

Carter had a beautiful neck and shoulders. No bony knobs or exaggerated cords. Solid and curved, looking as though he'd been sculpted by an artist. She'd told him how much she enjoyed looking at his shoulders once, but he hadn't taken her seriously, so she'd treated the whole thing as a big joke. But it hadn't been.

She drew her hand away, annoyed with herself. Fondling an unconscious man. And not just any man, but a man who had made it plain that he didn't want her.

How pathetic. The thought gave her the impetus she needed to return to the pilothouse.

She could hear Saunders's voice squawking through the radio as soon as she approached the helm.

Nikki grabbed the microphone. "This is Honey Bee WZB 6195. How ya doin', Saunders?"

"Nikki!" There was silence and Nikki imagined Saunders catching his breath. "I was beginning to worry."

Beginning to worry? Nikki smiled. "Did you think he'd thrown me overboard?"

"Yes."

She laughed before pressing the transmit button. "Relax, Saunders. He's still asleep."

"Uh . . ."

She guessed Saunders wanted to ask if she'd told Carter that he was still married. Julian was likely within earshot. "I briefed Carter as you advised," she said, hoping Saunders understood. "He wants to discuss everything later. How's damage control on your end?"

Julian responded. "The Karrenbrocks are going with the appendicitis story. Dee Ann is supposedly keeping vigil at the groom's hospital bedside."

"Very noble of her, but doesn't she wonder where the hospital is? What did you tell her?"

"Nothing. We can't find her."

Nikki wasn't surprised. If she'd been jilted, she'd have hidden away, too, and not waited around enduring everyone's sympathy. "You did tell somebody *something*, didn't you?"

"Not exactly," Julian drawled.

This did not sound good. The plan had been hastily executed and rough spots were to be expected. It sounded as if they'd run into one of them. "What do you mean? Dee Ann and her family are probably frantic with worry."

"Not worried enough to call off the reception."

"*Dee Ann* was at the reception?"

"No, but everyone else in the wedding party was."

"You're kidding." Nikki looked over her shoulder to see if Carter was eavesdropping. She was alone. "With the groom in the hospital, they're partying?"

"Why not? Everything's already paid for."

"But . . ." Nikki wasn't quite certain of the protocol in a jilting situation, but this approach didn't seem correct.

"Bob says the food was great. Real champagne."

"Bob went to the reception?" Where had the accountant found the nerve?

There was a short silence before Bob's defiant tenor sounded through the radio. "—had to feed my family. Who knows when they'll eat their next meal now that I'm unemployed?" Instead of releasing the microphone button, he continued to hold it down. Nikki couldn't answer him until he released the button, but she could hear everything.

"There, what did I tell you?" Bob complained to the others. "She has no answer. *She* doesn't have kids who depend on her to feed them. *She* won't have to tell them why Santa didn't—" There was a crackle of static, then silence.

Grinning, Nikki pressed the button. "Bob, Carter reinstated us."

"—long were you going to let me suffer before telling me?"

Nikki wanted to conk him on the head with the microphone.

Apparently, she wasn't the only one. Saunders was the next person to speak and she could hear Bob and Julian arguing in the background.

"Do you think it's safe for us to come out tomorrow?"

"I guess so." Actually, she'd be glad of the company. "Let me give you my location." They'd arranged a crude code earlier in case any hostile parties were monitoring the frequency. Nikki didn't think Victor Karrenbrock would suspect Carter was on a boat, but she didn't want to take any chances.

"Gotcha," Saunders said. "Can we bring you anything?"

Nikki thought for a moment, staring wistfully at the bobbing horizon. "Yeah, how about a couple of rib eyes and a head of lettuce?"

HE SMELLED FOOD.

Opening his eyes, Carter tried to get his bearings. Black, white and screaming yellow. He was still aboard the *Honey Bee*. It hadn't been a nightmare. He lifted his left hand, noted his ringless finger and groaned. Wrong. He'd awakened to a nightmare.

Bracing himself, he eased into a sitting position. His headache was nearly gone, but the rocking of the boat remained.

They were at anchor.

And he was hungry. Well, no wonder; it was nearly seven-thirty, he realized as he consulted the captain's wall clock. Blinking away the last remnants of sleep, he ran his fingers through his hair and assessed the situation.

Other than feeling as if he'd been hit by a truck, he didn't feel too bad.

He stood, testing his sea legs. After a slight initial wobble, Carter picked his way around the scattered files and entered the head. He'd live, he thought, and splashed his face with water.

Better and better. Now, he was ready to grill Nikki and grill her he would.

And speaking of grilling . . . Following his nose, Carter located her in the dinette just outside the galley. Bathed in the glow of a tiny portable television set, she was eating a solitary supper.

"What's that slop?" he said by way of greeting.

Nikki swept her cool green gaze over him and swallowed. "Dinner." Turning back to the television, she continued eating.

"It looks disgusting."

"I thought you'd be hungry after all this time. You'll feel more like eating in a few hours."

"I feel like eating right now." Carter slid onto the bench across from her.

Pointing with her fork, Nikki indicated the bookcase behind him. "Take your pick."

He looked behind him, but didn't see another plate. "What are you talking about?"

"Dinner. I think there's turkey and dressing, Salisbury steak, beef stew, sweet and sour—"

"I want real food!" he interrupted when he realized she was referring to the boxes he'd initially thought were books.

She shrugged. "Shelf-stable dinners. A great new product. No refrigeration necessary."

"You actually eat that stuff?" His stomach rebelled at the thought.

"Sure. Nuke it a couple of minutes in the microwave."

It seemed her standards had fallen since they'd last sailed together. "I'd prefer something fresh." Carter crossed his arms and waited.

Instead of jumping up to fix it for him, Nikki regarded him a moment, then cut off a chunk of Salisbury steak. "Here." She picked up a gravy-coated blob with her fingers and offered it to him.

Carter recoiled. "What's that for?"

"Bait. If you want fresh food, you'll have to catch it yourself."

"You're joking."

"Not at all." When he didn't take the meat, Nikki shrugged and popped it into her mouth. "We left in a hurry and I just grabbed a few things from my fridge before we headed to the church. If you're that desperate, you can scramble some eggs, but then there won't be anything for breakfast."

Carter tapped his fingers on the plastic-coated table top. "Eggs will be fine." Eggs were *not* fine, but he'd at least make a gesture of cooperation.

A gesture that was obviously lost on Nikki. She remained seated across from him, chewing on her unappetizing dinner. "Nikki," he said in his most reasonable voice. "I'm hungry now."

"Everything in the galley is still stored in the same place." She took a sip of something that looked like lemonade. "Oh, that's right. You didn't spend much time in the galley, did you." It wasn't a question.

At last, it dawned on Carter that Nikki was furious. Slowly, he rose to his feet. After all, *he* was the one entitled to be furious, wasn't he?

So she wouldn't cook for him. Fine. He wasn't completely helpless. Strolling into the compact galley, an architectural marvel of creative storage, Carter opened and closed cabinets and drawers, discovering nooks and crannies he'd never known about.

And if she thought he was going to feel the slightest bit guilty, she was wrong. No, he hadn't spent much time in the galley. That hadn't been his job. His job had been to . . . to relax and recharge so that he could perform at peak operating condition and continue to make enough money to support a boat like the *Honey Bee*, that's what his job had been.

He unearthed a small skillet and then spent a few moments familiarizing himself with the stove. It appeared to work on the same principle as a regular stove, not that he was familiar with those, either.

He jerked open the small refrigerator and stared at the eggs. They stared back.

"You're letting out all the cold air," Nikki said from behind him.

Carter shut the refrigerator door. He couldn't face eggs, after all. Pointedly replacing the skillet, he turned around.

Nikki lounged in the doorway. "I'll be topside, when you're ready to discuss business."

"Wait," he said when she started to leave. She raised an eyebrow. "You said something about stew?"

Nodding, she stepped over to the bookcase and flipped through the vertically shelved dinners. The proximity of food for the body and food for the mind drew a reluctant smile from Carter.

Nikki selected a square package and tossed it to him, then left the salon.

Ten minutes later, Carter stared at a respectable-looking beef stew. Why had Nikki made such a fuss about cooking for him? Open, heat and eat. Big deal.

He carried his plastic tray up the companionway steps and walked across the deck in time to enjoy the sunset as he ate his stew.

Nikki sat a level above him on the fly bridge, her feet propped on the railing. Carter hesitated. Nikki probably felt as sociable as he did right now.

Straddling a deck chair, Carter ate his stew. It was good, but that was probably because he was hungry. Tomorrow they'd eat fish, if this meat worked as bait.

No, *he'd* eat fish. Let Nikki catch her own.

During his solitary supper, Carter had avoided thinking. Now that he was pleasantly full and his head was no longer throbbing, it was time to straighten everything out. He did not look forward to it.

"Nikki?" he called.

Her voice drifted down to him. "Ready to talk business?"

Carter set his plate on the deck. "Business can wait." He swiveled until he could see her. "What's this about our still being married?"

"Yeah." After a moment, her feet disappeared and he heard her climb down.

Joining him on the deck outside the pilothouse, she flopped onto a chaise. "In the for better-or-worse category, this is definitely worse." She sounded—and looked—exhausted. It occurred to him that their present situation must be as difficult for her as it was for him.

"What about the divorce?" he asked. He remembered her trip to Mexico. They'd both wanted it over as quickly and as discreetly as possible.

Nikki adjusted the back of the chair so that it reclined at a greater angle, then laced her hands across her stomach and closed her eyes.

This was going to be a long explanation, Carter surmised.

"When Saunders was drawing up your prenuptial agreement with Dee Ann, he asked me for a copy of our divorce decree so he'd know the date it became final," she began with a tired sigh. "We had to figure out the exact value of your stock."

"And?"

"I couldn't find the actual decree."

"Saunders has access to my personal legal papers. There should have been a copy somewhere," he said.

She turned her head without raising it from the chaise. "*You* don't have it, either."

"I've got *something*." It was true that he hadn't read the document carefully, but then, there had been more written in Spanish than in English.

Nikki sighed. "What we have is a copy of the letter the lawyer in Mexico filed with the Mexican government. So I suppose that in Mexico, we're divorced. Unfortunately, he never filed anything in the United States."

"So? You don't have to notify every country in the entire world when you get a divorce."

"No, but we were married in the United States and until the government is otherwise informed, our contract of marriage is still valid," she recited.

It was so simple. And so cataclysmic. "Oh... my... God."

"Exactly." Nikki closed her eyes again. "Go ahead and have a breakdown. I'll wait."

Carter stared at the sinking sun. Waves slapped the boat. Gulls soared above, searching for fish and debris. The muddy water of the gulf took on a golden hue and the humid sea air brushed against his face.

How could everything be so picturesque when the bottom had just dropped out of his world? "So how long have you known?"

"About three weeks."

"And nobody told me?"

"Saunders thought he could straighten everything out before the wedding."

"Obviously, he didn't!"

"Nope."

Carter would have a word with Saunders. "With the salary I pay him, you'd think he would have noticed a small thing like a missing divorce decree."

"Carter." Nikki reached across the space between them and gripped his arm. "Saunders feels horrible. Nothing you can say will make him feel any worse than he does now."

"I'm going to try."

Her arm fell away as Carter surged to his feet and paced beside the railing, his shirt cuffs flapping. He rolled them up his arms, then clutched the railing until his knuckles were white.

"Why didn't you tell me yesterday? Or early this morning?" He smacked the railing with his fist and turned to face her. "Why all this?" he asked, waving his arms.

"Now things get complicated," she began, looking at him. "Your invitations had already been mailed. Saunders and I thought that if the worst happened and our divorce decree hadn't been granted by the time your wedding was supposed to take place, we'd tell you, and you and Dee Ann could still go through with the ceremony, then slip away to city hall and get married legally later. We thought it would be a story to laugh about with your grandchildren." She grinned hopefully at him.

"Ha-ha." Dee Ann would have loved that. *Dee Ann!* Carter groaned. Man, was he going to pay for this.

"But then Bob found out how much stock your future father-in-law had been buying," Nikki continued hastily, "and that, coupled with the other activity, warranted some concern."

"And you expressed that concern. Repeatedly. But the fact remains, that Belden Industries is named *Belden* Industries, not Morrison Industries or Saunders Industries or anything else. It should have been *my* decision, Nikki."

She sat up, her jaw set. "You were too caught up in all the wedding froufrou to make any kind of decision!"

Nikki had just overstepped the bounds of friendship. "I think your original plan of our simply proceeding with the ceremony and dealing with the legalities later was the right one."

Nikki stubbornly shook her head. "No. Saunders said the prenuptial agreement could have been interpreted in a way that would give Dee Ann ten percent of the stock even without a *legal* ceremony. So we made sure there wasn't a ceremony."

Carter's anger heated. "You're implying that she's marrying me for my stock?"

"No." Nikki started to say something more, then visibly caught herself. "Yes," she said firmly. "That's exactly what I'm saying." She tilted her chin upward with a defiance he wasn't accustomed to seeing from her.

This was absurd. Crazy. Nikki and the others had all gone over the edge. When was the last time they'd taken a vacation, for God's sake?

Carter took a deep breath and prepared to deliver a scathing retort. "You're nuts."

"Am I?"

"Aren't you?"

"I don't think so," she answered, appearing to give the possibility some thought. "You saw the files. It looks like someone is preparing to launch a hostile takeover. And we think it's Victor Karrenbrock."

"And I think you're all crazy. You're saying a man would give his daughter to me one week and take control of my company the next?"

Nikki inclined her head.

Carter started pacing again. It made no sense. He told her so.

"It makes perfect sense if you ignore the fact that he's Dee Ann's father," Nikki insisted. "He's a cutthroat competitor. You're vulnerable. He's got the means and you just outbid him on a prime contract. He knows you'll be away from the company on your honeymoon. Frankly, if Victor Karrenbrock didn't make a run for your company now, someone else might."

"He'd do that to his own daughter?" Carter heard the plaintive note in his voice.

Nikki shrugged. "Business is business."

Carter felt as if he'd just been sucker-punched. He didn't want to believe it. "You don't have proof."

"Right now, Bob, Saunders and Julian are holed up in a beach house with their laptops. They'll be out here tomorrow morning."

He started to protest again, then stopped. Bob, Saunders, Julian and Nikki had been with him for years. Hell, he'd *married* Nikki. He knew they were not alarmists.

And he usually wasn't so slow. Such deviousness was entirely within Karrenbrock's character. As for Dee Ann... well, yes, there had been a time or two when wedding preparations had run on longer than he'd planned. But that was because they'd pulled the whole show together in three months.

He supposed he'd been more out of touch than usual. He'd suspended the informal staff meetings and missed a lunch here and there.

A memory of seeing Nikki's stricken face, as he interrupted her to take a call from Dee Ann flitted through his memory.

Okay, but *someone* should have managed to alert him before he was supposed to walk down the aisle.

He approached Nikki, still uncertain if he should strangle her or kiss her. "Nikki, what if you're wrong? How could I ever make this up to Dee Ann? I *jilted* her."

Nikki looked as if she'd swallowed something sour. "We took care of that. We told everybody you got sick."

"What, food poisoning?"

"Wish I'd thought of that. No, I said appendicitis."

"Appendicitis?" he asked sharply. "You told Dee Ann I had *appendicitis?*"

Wide-eyed, Nikki nodded. "I told the wedding coordinator, and Julian says that's the story the guests were told."

All his anger came rushing back. He took a step toward her and unhooked his pants.

Nikki, still babbling, scooted back. "Dee Ann will understand—"

She broke off when Carter, his eyes never leaving her face, took another step toward her and unzipped his fly. He was livid. Speechless. Karrenbrock had nothing on her for deviousness.

Talk about cutting out the competition. That was what this broken wedding was all about.

He'd been nursing a viper in his bosom. All this time, Nikki had been waiting for the opportunity to exact revenge. Dee Ann, who had never harmed anyone, had been publicly humiliated. If Karrenbrock hadn't been after Carter's company before, he certainly would be now.

"What are you doing?" Nikki squeaked.

With one violent movement, Carter jerked his shirt-tail up and his pants down. "Remember this?"

5

"OBVIOUSLY NOT." With a sinking feeling, Nikki found herself inches away from an appendectomy scar.

Inches away from other things, as well, but she wouldn't dwell on them. "I assume the bride has seen your scar?"

Glaring at her, Carter pulled his pants back into place. "Don't tell me you didn't plan this whole thing as an elaborate revenge!"

His voice lashed her and Nikki was unbelievably hurt that he could think such a thing of her. There was a time when she'd devoted her entire life to him. As it was, she still spent all her waking hours and a few sleeping ones thinking of Carter and Belden Industries.

It was time to get a life.

A life beyond Carter.

So she mentally cauterized her emotional wound and talked past the lump in her throat. "Give me some credit, Carter. If I'd wanted revenge, I would have taken my story to Dee Ann, not to you. And while this might come as a shock, I haven't spent the past three years dwelling on the intimate details of your body." She looked him up and down as she prepared for the coup de grace. "It wasn't that memorable."

She had the momentary satisfaction of seeing Carter

speechless. Then, clutching the waistband of his pants, he turned and stalked off.

Nikki knew she should feel absolutely terrible.

But she didn't.

SHE DID FEEL GUILTY the next morning, though, and cooked breakfast for Carter as a peace offering. After all, he was still her boss and it was hard to avoid him on the forty-foot boat. But it *was* possible, and so far this morning, Carter was succeeding. She could hear him rumbling around and knew that he'd showered.

Eggs and muffins should lure him out. She would fry bacon, if she had it, but she hadn't bought bacon since she and Carter had split up.

Saunders and the others were due in abo 't an hour, depending on how much time Julian had to spend reassuring Bob and how many boating mistakes Saunders made because he was nervous about the impending confrontation.

Nikki sighed and flipped the eggs. Carter liked them over-easy, which was the hardest way to cook them, she thought.

One yolk broke and yellow leaked around the edges. Rats. Nikki started to separate that egg from the other to discard it so she could try again for an unbroken yolk, then stopped herself. There was nothing wrong with the egg. It was still edible. That should be good enough for Carter.

The hair on the back of her neck prickled and she turned around. "You're just in time for—"

Carter, looking dangerous with his unshaven face and bare chest, stood in the doorway. He wore the *Honey Bee* swim trunks she'd had made.

"—breakfast," she finished at a higher pitch.

His gaze swept over both her and the eggs. "Oh, *please* don't go to any trouble on my account," he said, his voice heavy with sarcasm. "I'll cook my own eggs."

"These are for you. I usually have fruit and a muffin for breakfast."

"In that case, thank you." He gestured down at his attire. "You'll forgive me for not dressing. This was all I could find."

Clothes. No one had packed clothes for Carter. Well, she couldn't think of everything. "Sorry."

"You should be."

Now she wasn't. Not a bit. "For what? Saving you from making a huge mistake? From *bigamy?*"

Carter gave her a dark look and took the frying pan into the dinette. He scraped the eggs onto the plate. The other yolk broke.

"I'll get the coffee," Nikki said and escaped into the galley.

He was eating the eggs when she returned and set a mug in front of him. "Thanks," he said and wrapped his hands around it.

Nikki broke apart her bran muffin as he took a sip, grimaced, then took another sip.

"Is this decaf?"

"No. But it is skim milk," she admitted when he took another sip.

Glowering, he set the mug on the table. "I don't suppose you have cream?"

Nikki shook her head. "Just the powdered kind."

He sighed and finished his eggs.

What a lovely start to the morning, Nikki thought. If he remained this surly, they'd never convince him he had cause to be worried.

He didn't eat his bran muffin, either.

"I've scheduled a meeting this morning," Nikki informed him. "With Saunders, Julian and Bob, since he's the accountant most familiar with the stock activity."

Carter's head shot up. "You expect me to meet *anybody* looking like this?"

"I thought you'd want to shave first."

"With what? And don't offer me any razor you've used on your legs."

"I ought to, just to watch you bleed!"

"Stabbing me in the back wasn't enough?"

She grinned. "I know what you're doing. You're powerless in this situation—"

"Ha!"

"—and so you're striking out. I'm simply the only available target."

Carter dropped his crumpled napkin by his plate. "And you say more targets are arriving shortly?"

Nikki was ahead of him. "Don't think you can commandeer their boat, either. I'll call the Coast Guard and report it stolen."

"And I'll report that I'm being held against my will."

They glared at each other, then Carter stood. Nikki stood, as well. It wasn't good negotiating practice to let your opponent tower over you. Of course, Carter was taller, but Nikki was wearing more clothes.

And they were on her boat. She had the power, so she offered a concession. "Tell you what. If you listen to us, and I mean *really* listen, Carter, and then still want to go ashore, I'll sail you in myself."

"Deal," he said at once.

Carter was a businessman. Nikki knew he'd realize this was the best he'd get. "Okay. In the guest cabin, there should be a plastic bag with toiletries. There ought to be a razor, toothbrush, toothpaste, that sort of thing. You can either change back into your wedding clothes, or I'll lend you one of the T-shirts I use for swimsuit coverups."

"One with little fishies?"

Nikki swept him a cool glance. "I'll find you something appropriate."

"I'd even take the fishies as long as I don't look like a damn bumblebee!" was Carter's parting shot.

"AHOY, Captain! Permission to come aboard."

Nikki had never been so glad to hear Julian's amused drawl in her entire life. "Permission enthusiastically granted!" she called back.

Even though Carter hadn't come back topside, the tension onboard the *Honey Bee* was as thick as, well, honey. Nikki had been sitting at the helm fretting about the files she'd left scattered on the floor of the master stateroom. She'd practically chained herself to the captain's chair to keep from retrieving them. Carter had strewn them about during his little tantrum yesterday evening. Let him pick them up. She was no longer his personal slave.

Funny, she'd never felt like a personal slave until he'd announced his engagement to Dee Ann. She'd enjoyed taking care of all the minute details of Carter's life and freeing him to concentrate on the myriad business dealings he always had cooking. She'd felt as if she was an integral part of the team.

However, in the past few weeks, she'd come to resent her role. She'd felt used. And the unaccustomed resentment on her part had polluted their carefully crafted relationship.

She helped Julian secure the motorboat to the *Honey Bee* and hauled up the cooler of provisions she'd asked them to bring.

Julian, in his white shorts and knit shirt, was casually elegant, as usual. Saunders, too, wore shorts, though he really didn't have the legs for them.

Glinting with gold braid, Bob appeared to have given himself the rank of admiral of a small European navy, then dressed for an inspection by visiting royalty.

Blinding white from head to toe, he'd somehow managed to keep his pants and jacket—the poor man must be sweltering in this heat—crisp. His foot slipped on the metal ladder because his shoes were hard-soled white patent leather.

Nikki rescued him, and started to say something, when Saunders gripped her arm in warning. "Are we meeting in the salon, Nikki?"

"Uh, yes."

"I'll take the cooler down to the galley and join you there. Come on, Bob." Saunders clapped the accountant on his braided shoulder. "Let me give you a tour of this sweet little boat."

Nikki stared after them before turning to help Julian.

Tying up the lines, Julian caught Nikki's eye and shook his head.

"Couldn't he at least lose the hat?" she murmured.

"Says it's protecting his scalp from the sun," Julian replied with a glance over his shoulder.

"Carter's in a foul mood," she warned him. "He'll probably say something awful."

"Bob's determined to show his respect. Saunders and I will draw Carter's fire."

"Wait until you see Carter."

Julian tied off the last rope, bent and tossed her a duffel bag. "I brought him some clothes," he said, climbing aboard.

"Bless you," she said fervently, waiting until he was on deck. "Let's go find the others."

"Nikki?" Julian touched her arm. "Are you okay?"

"I'm fine," she answered brightly, as if to reassure herself as much as Julian.

"Really?"

The quiet concern in his voice touched her. She smiled and nodded. Julian was a good friend. Admiring the handsome picture he made, she idly wondered why she wasn't the least bit attracted to him. "Carter's grumbling, but I think that'll stop if we can convince him he's in trouble."

"No problem there."

"More companies connected with Karrenbrock?" Even though it was what they'd all suspected, Nikki still felt a jolt at hearing Julian's confirmation.

"Yep. Come on," he said, a hand across her shoulders. "Admiral Bob will tell you all about it."

Admiral Bob stood at attention in the salon. Nikki briefly tried to get him to relax before Carter made his grand entrance.

It was a typical Carter ploy. He would allow everyone to assemble, become a little on edge, then sweep into the room, thump his materials at the head of the table, place one hand on either side and lean forward.

Only when Carter Belden arrived did things happen. It was an effective power play. He stood, they sat. He talked, they listened. He directed, they followed.

Nikki, Saunders and Julian had seen it all before. Bob was still a few rungs below the rest of them, and thus more in awe of Carter than they were.

Right now, Bob couldn't figure out where to sit. The salon boasted built-in padded sofas along the edges and two club chairs in front of the bookcases. The dinette was on the other side and had an elongated table between two benches. When they needed the sleeping space, Nikki lowered the table so it fit between the benches, and had another double bed.

"Bob, could I get you something to drink? Ice tea? Lemonade? Coffee?" She took in his stiff posture. "Scotch?"

"No!" Bob squeaked.

Saunders, who had been exploring the contents of the tiny bar, poured himself something dark and straight, and relaxed on a sofa. "Have a seat, Bob."

Bob's gaze darted from Saunders, guzzling liquid courage, to Julian, who, hands clasped behind him, was examining either the book titles or the available dinners on the shelves.

Bob, clutching his briefcase, edged toward Saunders.

"I'll take the lemonade, Nikki," Julian said, breaking the silence. "It's a lemonade kind of day."

Saunders drained his glass and lurched up to pour another.

Actually, Nikki thought as she dug out ice, it was more a scotch kind of day. And to top it off, at some point, she was going to have to engineer a time when Saunders could speak with Carter privately about the status of the divorce.

Handing Julian his lemonade, Nikki perched on the opposite end of the settee from Saunders who had obtained a second drink and was sitting there sipping it.

For a time, the only sounds in the salon were from the muted waves outside, and the clink of ice cubes inside.

It was into this pool of tension that Carter splashed. He strode into the salon, his gaze scouring the room. Nikki noted a momentary hesitation before he headed to the tiny dinette table and thumped the blue folder on it, his indication that the meeting was called to order.

"Ooh, Nikki," Julian whispered. "Like that T-shirt."

Saunders swallowed audibly.

And then Carter saw Bob. The two men stared at each other. *Be kind, Carter*, Nikki pleaded silently.

Bob tried to blend in with the decor, but only Carter truly succeeded, attired as he was in leftover *Honey Bee* upholstery.

Barefoot, he wore her favorite T-shirt—the one that said, A Woman's Place is in the House—and in the

Senate. Behind him, stuffed into a corner, was the bag of clothes Julian had brought aboard. An imp of mischief had prompted Nikki to keep that knowledge to herself.

Carter and Bob made an interesting contrast, yet no one who saw the two of them would be in any doubt about who was in charge.

"Good morning," Carter said, finally, to the nautical glory that was Bob.

Bob saluted.

"At ease, sailor," Carter said and opened the folder. "I've had a chance to review the data that you all found so urgent." As he spoke, he shuffled through the wrinkled papers. "Nikki informs me that you were still researching the companies involved in recent stock trading. Report?"

"Take it away, Admiral." Julian gestured to Bob.

Bob flushed and laid his briefcase on the dinette table.

Nikki had to give him credit. He remained standing, as did Julian, thus depriving Carter of one of his intimidation moves.

Carter stood just under six feet, but carried himself with such presence that he appeared taller. This time, with Bob wearing shoes and the hat, Carter found himself looking up at his head accountant.

He did not look pleased.

Bob launched into his report, guaranteed to further displease Carter. "In addition to Lacefield Foods and their three percent, we discovered that Medlock Chemical, in Ohio, and its subsidiary, Lucas Properties, owns four percent. Medlock's parent company is Karrenbrock Ventures."

Carter's face was blank and Nikki knew he was mentally doing the math.

"Also in the last ninety days," Bob continued when no explosion was forthcoming, "Karrenbrock bought SKS Manufacturing. They owned two percent. And we found . . . actually, Julian remembered," Bob said, apparently struggling to be scrupulously correct, "that Galit Industries sold off its oil-field services group and changed its name to Wright Equipment Corporation."

Everyone looked at Julian. He shrugged. "I went to their Christmas party."

"So, Wright, even though it hasn't appeared on the latest list of shareholders owns—"

"Stock," Carter finished. "I gave Galit some in exchange for machinery years ago. How much does Wright currently own?"

"Three percent," Bob answered.

Carter inhaled through his teeth. "Remind me to pay a call on the new CEO of Wright Equipment Corporation."

Bob darted a scared glance around the room, obviously losing his newfound nerve.

Saunders filled the breech. "Wright Equipment Corporation is a brand-new subsidiary of Karrenbrock Ventures. The ink isn't even dry on the new stationery."

The *Honey Bee* rocked slightly. Carter grabbed the table and sat heavily on the bench where his lower body disappeared into the stripes.

Nikki knew Bob's recitation had unnerved Carter. Even she hadn't expected it to be this bad.

Swallowing, Bob continued, "John Karrenbrock, Victor's son, has personal holdings of four percent—"

"How did that get by you?" Carter exploded.

Bob flinched and knocked his briefcase to the floor.

As Julian and Saunders defended everyone, Nikki crossed the salon to help Bob gather his papers. "He's not mad at you, he's mad at himself," she whispered. "Keep going."

Bob smiled weakly, perspiration dampening his shirt collar. "Am I still employed?"

"If you aren't, we'll see to it that you get the world's greatest severance package."

That calmed him down.

When they stood, Carter was scowling, his fist resting on the table.

"John Karrenbrock is doing business as JK Interests," Saunders was explaining. "So far, those interests haven't taken a tangible form."

"It's just a smoke screen for Karrenbrock to control more stock," Nikki said.

Carter slowly turned his head. "Is that all?" he asked Bob.

"So far."

"We concluded he'd make any overt moves, such as a buyout offer, this coming week," Saunders added. "By the time you could be reached and could react, it would all be over."

"Give me a bottom line."

Bob opened his mouth.

"Let me." Nikki snatched the paper from the accountant. For reasons she couldn't fully fathom, she wanted to be the one to deliver the news. "As it stands now, through family, companies and personal holdings, Karrenbrock controls thirty percent to your forty-nine. Marry Dee Ann and it drops to thirty-nine."

Carter looked up at her, an unidentifiable emotion flickering in the depths of his hazel eyes.

Julian sauntered over to join the rest of them at the tiny dinette table. This time, Carter sat and they all stood, surrounding him. Julian planted both fists on the table and leaned forward in blatant imitation of Carter's favorite stance. "And guess who'd be sitting in the driver's seat? Your wife and her ten percent."

Carter's eyes flicked to Nikki. She kept her expression stony.

Julian, clearly still bitter at being dumped by Dee Ann, was just warming up. "I can see it now...Honey, I want that mink at Neiman's or I'll vote with Daddy," he said in a singsong voice. He chuckled without mirth. "Oh, Carter. Just think. Before every crucial vote, you'd have to dance to her tune. You don't dare deny her anything. You won't own Belden—"

"Julian!" Nikki interrupted, worried about the brick color in Carter's face. "He didn't marry Dee Ann. Perhaps now he'll renegotiate the prenuptial agreement."

"Nikki." Carter spoke quietly, the color receding from his face. "I appreciate your running interference, but I take full responsibility for the consequences of my actions." He stood.

Nikki waited for praise. She waited for an apology. She waited in vain.

"In spite of the overwhelming evidence, I'm not willing to condemn my future father-in-law."

"What?"

"Carter—"

"How can you—"

They all spoke at the same time, like a Greek chorus spouting doom.

Even the unflappable Julian gasped before recovering his poise. "In that case, I'll polish up my résumé."

The most damning action came from Bob. He threw his admiral's hat on the floor, then defiantly unbuttoned his jacket.

"Calm down," Carter exhorted them, hands outstretched. "I still think Karrenbrock planned to give us stock as a wedding gift. I'd mentioned trying to increase my holdings—"

Saunders swore and headed back to the bar.

Carter stared them all down. "I will not believe that Dee Ann had any knowledge of her father's business dealings. She doesn't care about any of that."

Nikki tried to visualize Dee Ann. She'd met her before the wedding, but the only image she could recall was the blonde in her wedding dress as she stepped over the threshold on the arm of her father.

"Carter, you poor schmuck, she used me to get to you." Hand in his pocket, Julian faced him, twirling the leftover ice in his glass. "Obviously, it had all been planned from the start. She pursued me and I'll admit it. I was flattered and completely sucked in. Then the instant I introduced you two, she sent me for a glass of champagne and that was the last I saw of her. I looked like a complete fool, wandering around with two glasses of champagne until someone took pity on me and mentioned that she'd left the party with you."

Nikki knew the story. In fact, she was the someone who'd taken pity on Julian. Then she'd drunk that second glass of champagne and commiserated with him.

Carter took a step forward, his fists planted at his waist, his feet apart. He was, Nikki realized, literally making himself bigger, like some jungle animal staking out his territory. Julian was taller, but Carter was stronger.

And then Carter spoke. "Dee Ann's quite a woman, Julian. And once she met me, you weren't man enough to hold her interest."

Somebody was going to throw a few punches. It might even be Nikki.

But Julian was elegant, even in his anger. His icy gray eyes shifted to Nikki, warmed slightly in reassurance and returned to Carter. Then he set his glass on the dinette table with a precise chink, turned on his heel and left the salon.

Nikki *was* going to punch somebody.

Bob was a one-person tableau of horror. His skin color nearly matched that of his uniform and his mouth was a frozen O.

Saunders drained his glass. "Was she worth it, Carter?"

Carter didn't respond, just stared after Julian.

"I'll set a course back to Galveston," Nikki informed them, injecting her voice with as much acid as she could.

Let him marry Dee Ann and lose his company. Nikki no longer cared.

She, too, would have to polish up her résumé, she thought, climbing on deck.

Julian stood at the railing and instead of charting her course immediately, Nikki joined him.

"Dee Ann's a fool," she said.

Julian favored her with a half smile. "And why is that?"

"Because you're quite a catch."

"Am I?" He turned and leaned one elbow on the railing. "Then why haven't you gone fishing?"

"Because I—" *Because I'm the wrong kind of bait*, Nikki had begun to say until the expression on Julian's face registered. Much more than fondness lit his gray eyes.

Oh, no. She felt her muscles freeze, and her jaw drop, but she was powerless to do anything about it. Not Julian.

Well, why not Julian?

He was extremely good-looking and always dressed with care. He had proven his cleverness in countless sticky situations and his loyalty and integrity were unshakable.

In his own way, Julian was as formidable a businessman as Carter. Carter preferred to meet situations head-on and overpower them. Julian's way was more subtle, but just as effective.

In a fight, she'd want Julian in her corner. And hadn't he been there for her during yesterday's wedding fiasco?

Nikki desperately wanted to feel something for this man. She *liked* Julian. She imagined his well-shaped lips on hers, imagined the kind of lover he'd be.

And felt absolutely nothing.

Her eyes stung and filled.

With a bittersweet smile, Julian reached out with one long finger and tipped her jaw closed. "Because you're in love with Carter," he said, completing her sentence for her.

I'm not in love with Carter. Nikki would have given anything to be able to say the words. But she couldn't.

Julian gently caressed her cheek before withdrawing his hand and turning back to the sea. "It's all right, Nikki. Don't give it another thought."

There was nothing to say. Feeling absolutely wretched, Nikki left him there and stumbled into the pilothouse. All this time, she thought she'd fooled everyone about her feelings for Carter. She gazed wistfully at Julian. She was very fond of him, but it wasn't enough and they both knew it.

Less than a minute later, Bob appeared topside. When Saunders and Carter didn't join him, Nikki figured they were discussing the status of the divorce.

She would have preferred to hear the news from Saunders directly instead of depending on Carter for the information she needed.

Nikki was preparing to pull anchor when Saunders and Carter appeared on deck. Carter approached Julian. "Julian," he began, clasping his friend's shoulder, "this has all been very disturbing and if I said anything in the heat of the moment that offended you, I apologize."

Typical Carter, though she had to give him credit for making the first move. He wanted to put everything right, but truly did not feel that he'd done or said anything for which he should be sorry. It was a power apology.

She was saddened. After all these years, she'd have thought Carter would realize he could stop playing power games when he was around them. Granted, Bob was not part of the inner circle, but weren't the rest of them closer to Carter than mere employees? He always told them they were—when he wanted them to work around the clock on some project. Nikki handled the finances, Saunders the legal end and Julian was the front man.

"I'm pulling anchor!" she yelled before returning to the pilothouse to reposition the *Honey Bee*.

"Nikki!" Carter waved her over. "I've decided we'll stay anchored here for a few more days," he announced. "We'll monitor stock activity on Monday and Tuesday and formulate a plan if we need to."

Nikki interpreted that to mean that Saunders needed more time to untangle the divorce and that Carter was using the stock activity as a cover to remain onboard.

"Now, about Dee Ann," he said, avoiding looking at Julian. "She will, of course, know that I don't have appendicitis. Nikki, you're a woman, what explanation would be the most palatable for my leaving the wedding so suddenly?"

She looked him right in the eye. "Death."

He nodded as if considering. "Sounds plausible. Whose?"

"Yours."

They glared at each other.

Saunders cleared his throat. "I think severe stomach cramps due to food poisoning might be the way to go.

We—okay, I'll say *I* overreacted and thought it was appendicitis, and in the ensuing confusion...et cetera, et cetera."

"And in the event his beloved chooses to visit him?" Julian asked.

"He can't bear for her to see him like that," Saunders improvised. "Anyway, I took the liberty of sending her an obscenely expensive bouquet of roses with that sentiment and a suitably mushy—"

"*Roses?*" Carter roared. "You sent Dee Ann *roses* from me?"

Julian frowned. "Carter, it's hardly the time to begrudge a couple hundred dollars—"

"*Dee Ann is allergic to roses!*" Carter was quivering with rage.

Bob was merely quivering.

Nikki didn't know it was possible to look simultaneously delighted, yet appropriately shocked, but Julian managed it.

"Oh," was Saunders's contribution.

Carter, his jaw set, took a few deep breaths before disappearing below. A string of curses trailed after him.

"Well." Julian rubbed his hands together. "I suppose we should be getting under way, now." Bob scrambled to help him with the lines.

"Headache, Saunders?" Nikki asked, pulling him aside.

He winced. "I'll contact Dee Ann and tell her the roses were my idea."

"But then you'll have to explain where Carter is and why he didn't contact her himself."

He moaned. "I'd probably make the situation worse, though how can that be? The other matter," he said with raised eyebrows, "will take a while, even by calling in favors."

Now *she* had a headache.

"Coming Saunders?" Julian called. He and Bob were already in the motorboat and wearing life jackets.

Saunders climbed down the ladder. As he fastened his life jacket, Nikki cast off.

"We'll check in at eighteen hundred hours tonight," Julian said. "Good luck!"

"Cowards!" she called as they drifted away from the *Honey Bee*. "You're leaving a defenseless woman here to deal with Carter alone."

"If anyone can handle him, it's you, Nikki!" Julian flashed her a wide smile.

"We salute you," Saunders said, and as Julian revved the motor, that's exactly what they did.

6

IN SPITE OF HERSELF, Nikki laughed and returned their salute, then watched as the boat plowed through the water back to Galveston.

Roses. Dee Ann was allergic to roses. How... unfortunate. Now that she thought about it, Nikki remembered the carnation boutonnieres and the heavy scent of gardenias at the wedding. Nary a rose in sight.

She tried to feel as awful for Carter as she knew she should—and failed. After what she'd just heard below, Carter was well rid of the Karrenbrock clan.

However, she didn't expect Carter to share her views. She sighed, wondering how she could apologize to Carter. She also wondered if Julian knew Dee Ann was allergic to roses and suspected that he did.

She smiled, then frowned. This was not funny. She should practice being properly remorseful.

"They're gone?"

"Yes." Occupied with her facial gymnastics, she hadn't heard Carter come up behind her. "They abandoned ship."

Carter joined her at the railing as they both stared after the fast-moving speck.

Nikki glanced at him. He didn't seem to be in the grip of an uncontrollable rage. Now would be the time to apologize. She tried for a remorseful and repentant tone. "Carter, I'm truly sorry" *that we didn't think of this before* "about the roses. It's just one of those" *terribly funny* "things." She garbled the last word, her lips quivering with suppressed laughter. Maybe he'd think she was about to cry.

Carter wasn't buying any of it. "Assuming Dee Ann will ever speak to me again, what could I possibly say to her?"

"The truth?" Nikki batted her eyelashes at him.

Sighing, he gripped the railing. "I think not." Arms apart, he pulled on the boat's railing, peered over the edge, then turned and leaned with his back to the sea.

Nikki watched him as he studied the *Honey Bee* from bow to stern, taking in the teak trim against the gleaming white hull, the fresh varnish and shiny brass work.

The warm breeze ruffled his hair and to Nikki's eye, he appeared more relaxed than she'd seen him in days. The lines on his face weren't as pronounced and his mouth had lost the pinched look at the corners.

He actually smiled. "She's still a beauty."

Molten pleasure spread through Nikki. To hide it, she buffed at an imaginary smear on the handrail with her shirt.

"Forty feet is a lot of boat for a single person to handle," he commented. "I thought you were going to sell her."

Still buffing, Nikki lifted a shoulder. "Couldn't find a buyer." Not that she'd tried particularly hard. "Besides, there are a lot of memories tied up in this boat."

"All the more reason to sell her."

Nikki glanced up and away. Obviously, Carter was over any passionate feelings for her. "They weren't bad memories." That was his cue to agree with her.

"So you've kept this as an expensive souvenir of our . . ." He waved his hands mutely.

"Our marriage?" she emphasized. "Go ahead and say it, Carter. That's what we had, such as it was. Or is."

"One of my more unsuccessful mergers." He smiled with a wry attempt at humor.

Nikki was not amused. *A merger.* A business deal. That's the way Carter had thought of their marriage. Nikki imagined him drawing up a column of pros and cons, advantages and disadvantages, initial costs versus future estimated earnings, just the way he did before embarking on any business maneuver.

The golden haze through which she'd filtered her memories burned away. That's all she'd ever meant to him, she realized with new clarity. A plus in the pro column.

The *Honey Bee* was just like their marriage. Brass didn't shine on its own and the deck didn't varnish itself. Nikki was out here every other weekend doing routine maintenance to keep her boat seaworthy. It took work, just like a marriage did. But while Carter had been willing to enjoy the fun parts of marriage, he hadn't put in his share of the work.

Then again, Nikki hadn't allowed him to. She'd taken over everything herself, while at the same time becoming more and more resentful until one day, she'd had enough.

"Hey," he said. "If we're still married, then I still own half the *Honey Bee*, right? She's appreciated in value. I can get a better price for my half."

He couldn't have picked a worse time to make that remark. "Then I still own ten percent of Belden Industries, which reduces your personal holdings," she told him with cool confidence.

The smile was erased from his face. "What are you talking about?"

"I gave you four percent in exchange for your half of the *Honey Bee*, remember? Belden Industries has appreciated in value. Now, it'll cost you more to buy me out."

"That's not funny, Nikki."

"I wasn't trying to be funny."

"I was."

"I'm not laughing."

Carter stared at her as if seeing her for the first time.

In a way, he might have been. She'd presented only the cheerfully efficient Nikki to him at work and she'd carried that cheerful efficiency into their marriage. Carter's needs came first with her to the point that she'd unwisely submerged herself.

Mistakes. They'd both made mistakes.

Impulsively, she asked, "Are you in love with Dee Ann?"

"What made you ask that?" Carter replied with wariness.

He hadn't answered the question. Or perhaps his lack of an answer *was* an answer. Nikki felt lighter. "I was thinking about our relationship and how we'd both made mistakes and, well—" she chuckled "—Dee Ann came to mind."

Carter's nostrils flared. "I am *not* going to discuss Dee Ann with you."

Let him try his fire-breathing dragon act on somebody else. Nikki wasn't impressed. "Then I'm going to listen to the weather radio. Make yourself at home." She forced herself to walk away without looking back.

If Carter wanted a drink, she told herself, he knew where the bar was.

If Carter wanted something to eat, he knew where the galley was.

And if Carter wanted to nap, he'd nap alone.

CARTER WANTED to fish. "Nikki, is the fishing gear still stowed on board?"

"Yes," she called before disappearing into the pilot-house.

Grumbling to himself about the capricious nature of women, Carter went below.

The last he remembered, the fishing poles were strapped to the upper bulkhead in the bow. Two bunks were wedged in there for sleeping accommodations in a pinch or for kids who loved the compact slanted area.

What shape would the rods and reels be in? Carter visualized frozen gears, rusty hooks and knotted lines. Nikki never fished, or she hadn't used to.

Who knew what Nikki did nowadays? She wasn't the same Nikki he'd been married to—was *still* married to, he corrected.

He sighed in faint regret for the Nikki who had been. *This* Nikki had obviously overcome her case of hero worship and actually, he realized, it was a relief.

It had been lonely up on that pedestal.

Carter located the rods, exactly where he'd expected to find them. He couldn't tell if they'd been used in the past three years, but they were in great condition, just as everything was on the *Honey Bee*.

Had Nikki maintained the boat all by herself?

He had a sudden image of Nikki and someone else— a shirtless man, taller than him, with a flashing white smile and oiled pecs. Carter's hand tightened on the fishing rod and he just missed hooking himself.

Naturally, there would have been someone else, maybe even several someone elses, in the past three years. Nikki was young and attractive, but not too young or too attractive. Seasoned. She was smart and she had this sweet boat.

Men liked boats and women who knew their way around them.

Carter squatted in the bow, checked the fishing equipment and dealt with an entirely unwanted and unexpected surge of jealousy.

How absurd. Nikki was entitled to date men. Even marry them—after she finished divorcing him, that is.

Did she date?

Groping for the tackle box, Carter knocked loose the padding that kept it from banging against the retaining bar. The lumpy khaki material landed near his feet. He bent to retrieve it and recognized it as his fishing hat. "Hello, old friend. I'd forgotten all about you." He noticed the familiar pattern of stains, a fraying tear and the whitened ring bleached by his own sweat, then grinned and plopped the hat onto his head.

Nikki hated his hat.

Perfect.

Backing out of the bow, Carter's next stop was the dinette bookcase. "I wonder what sort of fish like Salisbury steak?" he muttered as he took one of the dinners and climbed two levels up to the flybridge. Big ones, he hoped.

Once on the fly bridge, he unrolled the canvas awning. More yellow, black and white, still in good condition. Why couldn't she have picked a nice marine blue?

As he worked, he saw Nikki leave the pilothouse and go below. There must not be any rough weather headed their way, which meant he could spend the rest of the afternoon fishing.

Carter dug in the tackle box for a penknife. Slitting open the dinner, he carved chunks of Salisbury steak and baited his hook. Casting his line, he watched the meat drop into the water below then secured the fishing rod in one of the holders along the side.

After baiting and casting his second hook, Carter settled into the chair and tilted his hat over his face.

Instantly, he relaxed, just as he had on countless other Sunday afternoons on this boat.

It was as if a missing piece of his life suddenly fit back into place and he felt content and whole once again, as he could only feel aboard the *Honey Bee*.

That's where he went wrong—letting Nikki buy his half of the boat. He should have offered to buy *her* out. In fact, he could still do so. Nikki was probably tired of all the maintenance work and would be grateful to him for taking the craft off her hands.

The decision to buy the *Honey Bee* felt good and solid. Carter reeled in his line and cast it again. By any right, he should be a man in turmoil, yet he felt at peace. The wedding and all its fuss was over. Time would tell if his relationship with Dee Ann was, as well.

And right now, he truly didn't care one way or the other. He wondered if Dee Ann felt the same way. He had no illusions about why she was marrying him—she wanted a certain life-style and he could provide it. But had she ever considered why *he* was marrying her? Did she think he was dazzled by her?

Propping his feet on the railing, Carter pondered the last three months. Within five minutes of his proposal, the Karrenbrock wedding machine had revved up.

It was as if they'd been expecting him to propose, even though he'd only been dating Dee Ann a matter of weeks. After that, he was sucked into the wedding whirlpool, the responsibility of approving Dee Ann's choice of china pattern taking on equal importance with negotiating steel prices.

He'd gone a little crazy there, he supposed.

Carter wondered what Dee Ann was thinking and decided he'd rather not know. It was kinder to let her believe that he was too ill to phone. Besides, he had no business trying to reconcile with Dee Ann until he was disentangled from Nikki.

Checking his lines, he was disappointed to see that he hadn't caught lunch yet.

His stomach rumbled just as a charred scent wafted up to him. Who was grilling?

Sitting upright, he pushed back his hat and gazed around, searching for another anchored boat.

Nothing but sea gulls and oil rigs.

He inhaled deeply. The galley exhaust outlet was just below him, which meant Nikki was making those sublime smells.

Steaks. She always grilled steaks after sex.

A smile stole across his face. Sex with Nikki . . .

His *Honey Bee* swim trunks were suddenly too tight. He shifted, but it didn't help. The canvas material had no give in it. The more he moved, the worse it got.

His discomfort was all due to Nikki. He wouldn't be having this problem if it weren't for her. Today was supposed to be the second day of his honeymoon. He shouldn't have been sitting on a fly bridge with quite the same ache.

"Carter?" Nikki's head appeared.

Carter's feet dropped to the deck and his hat dropped to his lap.

"Have you caught anything yet?" She climbed up the ladder until she was standing on the fly bridge next to him, bringing the scent of her cooking with her. *Eau de Rib eye.*

"No," he managed to say.

Her legs were still her best feature. Long and lightly tanned, they seemed to go on and on before the frayed hem of her cutoffs topped them. It was an unexpected feature in one no more than medium height.

"Julian brought out more provisions. If you're willing to declare a truce, you can share my lunch," she offered, ducking under the awning.

"Are we at war?"

"You seem to think so."

"The past twenty-four hours have convinced me that I'm at war with *somebody*." He raised an eyebrow. "I just have to figure out who."

"'He who hesitates is lost,'" Nikki quoted, standing her ground on her very fine-looking legs. Carter remembered how those very fine-looking legs felt wrapped around his waist.

His hat moved.

"In that case," he said, carefully adjusting his position, "a truce is an excellent idea."

She gave him a bright smile that rivaled the white-hot Gulf of Mexico sun.

Carter started to melt.

"Ready for lunch?" she asked.

"Steaks?" he asked, though he knew exactly what she'd cooked.

"Rib eyes. Charred on the outside, rare in the middle."

Wrapped in smoke, her words hung in the sea air.

Carter inhaled. "Just the way I like them."

"I remember." She held his gaze, then lowered hers.

He felt it touch his mouth, linger at his shoulders, move down his chest and stop at his hat. His torso burned with an icy heat. His hands crumpled the hat brim.

Nikki's chest rose and fell.

And one of the fishing poles bobbed, then bent in an arc.

They both looked at it, then at each other.

"Looks as if you've caught your own lunch."

"No!" Carter said, too quickly. He reached for the pole. "This can be dinner."

He concentrated on reeling in his catch and keeping his hat in his lap. Overly conscious of Nikki's presence, he managed to lose the fish.

"Better luck next time." Turning, Nikki ducked out from under the awning. "Coming?"

Carter closed his eyes. "Not yet," he answered, his voice raspy.

"Whenever you're ready," she said, walking away.

He was ready *now*.

Finding that Nikki still had the power to arouse him shocked Carter. Nikki was an officer in his company. After the initial awkwardness following their separation, they'd successfully resumed a platonic working relationship. Julian hadn't thought Carter could pull it off, but he had.

There was nothing platonic, however, about the look she'd just given him.

It was being back aboard the *Honey Bee* together. This wasn't the same Nikki who wore suits to work. This Nikki wore cutoff shorts, droopy T-shirts and white deck shoes. An entirely different Nikki. It made sense that she'd act different, too. Freer. Sassier.

The *Honey Bee* had that effect on people, or at least on the two of them.

Carter stood, stuck his hat back on his head and climbed down from the fly bridge. Nikki, memories and the smoke in the salty air had conspired against him. It was a Pavlovian response. No big deal.

"It's too hot to eat outside," Nikki said when Carter finally made his way to the galley.

She brushed past him, carrying in bowls of salad. The steaks sizzled on the dinette table as Carter's skin sizzled from the unexpected contact with Nikki. A recently quelled throbbing began anew.

"Did you want wine with lunch?" she asked.

"No." He removed his hat. "Too early and too hot."

"Agreed," she said, sliding onto the bench. "I've got caulking to do this afternoon. I found a leak in one of the salon portholes." She smiled up at him and slid her napkin—more leftover *Honey Bee* stripes—onto her lap.

Carter was grateful for her easy chatter and peeved that she recognized the need for it. "Not the aft porthole on the starboard side again?" he asked, sitting opposite her. He picked up his *Honey Bee* napkin and draped it over his lap, making sure the stripes were going in the opposite direction from his trunks and the bench.

"The very one."

"I remember sealing it."

"And I sealed it again after you did. So now," she said, picking up a fork, "I think the leak is not actually in the porthole itself, but that water is getting in somewhere else, running along the interior wiring and dripping out nearby."

"Sounds like you're in for some tedious detective work," Carter said as he contemplated his steak. It was a well-cooked piece of meat. Nothing more. He'd eaten steak a hundred times since he was last aboard the *Honey Bee* and not once had he responded with *this* sort of hunger.

He heard Nikki's silverware scrape. She was eating her steak. What was she thinking?

"Julian brought us some fresh sourdough bread from that new bakery near his penthouse. Try some." She held a napkin-wrapped loaf out to him.

Sourdough bread wasn't on their special menu. Their menu was steak, salad and wine, eaten under the stars. For a moment, Carter felt betrayed, which was ridiculous.

"It was warm when he brought it on board," Nikki coaxed, still offering the bread.

Carter ripped a hunk off just to appease her, but the tangy yeast aroma made his mouth water. "Butter?"

Nikki wrinkled her nose. "Fat." She pulled off a tiny piece of bread and popped it into her mouth. "This is wonderful, fresh-baked bread. How can you bear to drown it in fat?"

"I like fat."

Nikki tugged off another piece. "You have plenty of fat right there," she said, pointing to his steak. "Savor the natural taste of the bread." She closed her eyes and chewed slowly, making little humming noises.

Looking askance, Carter bit into the bread. "Okay, it's good," he admitted. "But it would be great with butter."

Nikki opened her eyes, apparently finished savoring her bread. She eyed him speculatively. "So. What's the word on our divorce?"

Carter had been about to cut into his steak. Sighing, he set down his cutlery. "Saunders hasn't been able to locate your lawyer. It would have helped, Nikki, if you'd hired one with a last name other than Garcia. Garcias are the Smiths of Mexico."

"Saunders found him for me."

Saunders had failed to mention that bit of information. "Unfortunately, he can't find him now. So he's tried various judges in Mexico, but hasn't been able to locate a copy of our divorce decree. It's been more than three years and Saunders can't even read the judge's signature on the papers we do have."

"I told him to have a judge in this country issue a divorce decree, since that's all that's lacking."

Carter nodded. "That's what he's doing."

"So how much longer?"

"I don't know." She sounded even more eager than *he* did. His immediate reaction was hurt pride. His second was to wonder how his pride got involved. As far as he was concerned, they'd divorced more than three years ago, legal technicalities aside. "By the way, I'd appreciate you and Saunders keeping this to yourselves."

She sighed. "It hasn't been easy, especially since I could have used Julian's advice." Her eyes narrowed. "You were horrible to him, you know."

Carter knew, though he didn't want to admit it. It was unusual for Nikki to criticize him and he felt defensive. "I apologized."

"No, you didn't," she countered. "You played power games with him."

"Are you speaking as my wife or my employee?"

"I'm speaking as Nikki," she said simply.

Carter caught himself just before he asked who that was. She'd continued eating her steak and salad as he grappled with a startling revelation: he knew Nikki the wife and Nikki the comptroller. *He didn't know Nikki the person.*

He didn't know how she'd act, though he suspected he'd met her up on the fly bridge. He didn't know what opinions she held. He didn't know how to decipher the meaning behind her words.

Thunderstruck, he stared at the bent head of the woman seated opposite him—the woman who had been his employee for seven years. The woman to whom he'd been married for several months.

And he realized she was a complete stranger.

7

"WHAT'S THE MATTER?" Nikki glanced up in time to discover the most peculiar expression on Carter's face. If she didn't know better, she'd think he was seasick.

"I—you're right about Julian. I was still angry. I knew he'd been seeing Dee Ann when I met her, but she never indicated that there were any strong feelings on either side. Julian dates a lot of women. I didn't realize Dee Ann's desertion rankled."

"It did."

Nikki tore off a chunk of bread. It had cooled, but was still wonderful. "You need to tell Julian this. You can't leave things as they are between the two of you. You realize that you're very lucky to have Julian, don't you?"

"And he's amply rewarded," Carter said, a hint of warning in his voice.

"Carter." Nikki set down the bread. "Julian's the sort of man who wants more out of life than money or a title. He could easily run his own company. At the very least, he could run someone else's company. He's had offers, you know."

"No." Carter blinked. "I didn't know."

Gratified to see Carter surprised, Nikki continued. "And for a better title and salary, too."

"He never said anything to me."

"He wouldn't." Nikki sighed and leaned forward. "Carter, you're a compelling, dynamic man and people love to work for you. You ask a lot, but after a big project, you come in and high-five everybody from the receptionist to your vice presidents, and make us feel that you couldn't have done it without us."

"But I couldn't have," he said with the utter sincerity that his employees sensed.

It was one of his endearing qualities. Carter had plenty of endearing qualities; he just kept them hidden most of the time. Only those who knew him well ever saw his small vulnerabilities.

"The four of us make a great team." Almost like a family, Nikki thought. "Julian would miss that if he worked somewhere else."

"How do you know all this?" Carter asked.

Nikki sat back. "Because I know Julian. Don't you?"

"Apparently not." He twirled his fork, clearly ill at ease.

"Shall I reheat your steak?" she offered.

"No. Thanks." He cut into it, but Nikki could see that his thoughts were elsewhere—with Julian, she hoped.

Carter brought the piece of steak to his mouth. "This is good. You haven't lost your touch, Nikki."

She smiled. "Brings back memories, doesn't it?"

He regarded her thoughtfully. "What memories were you trying to bring back?"

She gave him a sultry smile. "The good ones."

His eyes widened and she nearly laughed aloud. Poor Carter didn't know how to react. It made her feel powerful and in control for once.

He placed his knife and fork carefully on the plate. "Nikki . . ."

"Oh, pooh, Carter. Relax." She stood and carried her dishes into the galley, intending to leave him with his thoughts. "I'm going to chase down that leak," she called. "Since I cooked, you can clean up."

Carter in a kitchen, what a laugh. Nikki didn't actually know if he would wash the dishes. He never had before. There wasn't enough room in the galley for two people to work without bumping into each other.

No, that wasn't true. There was plenty of room for one to wash and one to dry.

Nikki opened the door to the engine room and climbed down the ladder. She'd promised herself that she wasn't going to act as Carter's personal servant on this trip. She didn't make his coffee at the office; there was no reason to wait on him now. Yes, their circumstances were unusual. Yes, Nikki found herself wanting to take care of Carter. But he'd chosen someone else to act as his wife. She needed to remember that.

As she found and loaded the caulking gun, Nikki acknowledged that this weekend with Carter was necessary for her peace of mind. Her trip to Mexico for their divorce had been hastily planned—too hastily, as it turned out—and she'd never really felt her relationship with Carter had ended. They'd been so intent on preserving their working rapport, that there had been no blowup, no final argument. They'd separated because she'd pressed for more emotional closeness than he could give, and he'd backed off. Way off.

They had unfinished business.

Serenaded by the hum of the generator, Nikki stood in the harsh shadows cast by a single lightbulb. Although she'd filed for divorce, she hadn't believed their marriage was over. Couldn't believe it when he announced his engagement to Dee Ann. Never expected him to go through with the ceremony.

Why would he turn to Dee Ann when Nikki was right there? What could Dee Ann give him that Nikki couldn't? Or hadn't?

What could she have done differently?

Her hand tightened on the caulking gun and a white glob oozed out the tip.

She couldn't let go of their marriage until she knew what had gone wrong. And before they returned to shore, she intended to find out.

CARTER CLIMBED back onto the fly bridge a firm believer in paper plates. Washing dishes was a waste of good fishing time.

He knew what Nikki was doing—punishing him for his remarks to Julian. He doubted Julian was suffering any such punishment.

How did Carter get to be the bad guy in this escapade? There he was, minding his own business—which was getting married—when they kidnapped him.

Was it *his* fault Nikki and Saunders had bungled the divorce? No.

Was it *his* fault they had failed to notice the possible takeover earlier? Couldn't a man get married without his company falling apart?

Fish had stolen the bait off both hooks. At least he knew they'd eat it. After rebaiting his hooks, Carter slouched in the deck chair. He ought to be studying the papers Bob had left, but he didn't want to.

It was hot out here, and when he couldn't stand the heat any longer, then he'd retire to the salon or the master stateroom.

His gaze was caught by a white-shirted figure in a floppy hat. Nikki was searching for her leak. Using a set of storage steps, she examined the joints just underneath the upper deck. Apparently finding nothing, she hopped off the steps and moved them a couple of feet toward the bow.

How could she stand this heat?

As he watched, she used a putty knife to dig out some old caulking compound around one of the salon windows. Reaching overhead caused her full shirt to inch upward, exposing familiar black, white and yellow strips.

Nikki had changed from her shorts and was now wearing her *Honey Bee* swimsuit.

Carter groaned. How precious they must look. He hoped they wouldn't encounter anyone they knew. Involuntarily, he scanned the horizon. The embarrassment of being caught dressed like an advertisement for wine coolers would be the least of his worries. How could he explain his presence on the *Honey Bee* when he was supposed to be in the hospital?

Fortunately, other Sunday sailors were keeping their distance and not venturing this far out into the gulf.

The scrape of Nikki moving the steps drew his attention. It looked as if she was unscrewing the window frame. Several times, she swiped at her forehead with her sleeve, then, to Carter's consternation, she dropped the screwdriver and peeled off her shirt, revealing her swimsuit. And her body in the swimsuit.

She was still winning the battle against gravity, Carter noted with a dry swallow.

Nikki's two-piece suit, designed as a companion to his, was cut high on the thigh, lengthening her already incredible legs. Her stomach was still flat and her arms had more muscle definition than he remembered. Nikki had been working out.

Carter sucked in his gut, mentally resolving to increase his trips to the company gym.

It was *hot* out here. He should have brought something to drink with him.

Nikki finished unscrewing the window frame and he saw her look around as if searching for something. Finally, she took off her hat and emptied her hand into the crown. The screws. She'd been looking for someplace to put them.

Now that Nikki wasn't wearing the hat, Carter could see down her strapless top. There was nothing there he hadn't seen before, but for some reason, he felt like a voyeur. It was no surprise to feel his suit grow tight again.

Sighing, he shifted. Nikki jumped off the steps with a bounce, then bent over to retrieve her caulking gun.

Carter moaned and closed his eyes.

He absolutely, positively, unquestionably and without a doubt, should *not* be thinking of Nikki this way.

There, sitting on the fly bridge above her, Carter called himself every vile name he could think of. He was *engaged*. About as close to married as a man could get and not actually *be* married. To another woman. To

Dee Ann. Visualize Dee Ann, he told himself. Visualize Dee Ann on board the *Honey Bee*.

He couldn't. In desperation, Carter tried to visualize Dee Ann wearing the damn *Honey Bee* suit.

And couldn't.

Tried to visualize Dee Ann's breasts. And could. Unfortunately, they suffered by comparison.

Good God almighty, a woman was more than her breasts! With self-loathing, Carter shoved his hat over his face.

He ached. It was a just punishment.

Mentally lusting after another woman . . . could he possibly be excused because he was married to that other woman? Was that the problem? If he weren't married, Nikki would merely be a good-looking woman in a swimsuit, one he could appreciate academically. Impersonally. Yes, that was it.

Carter pushed the hat away from his eyes.

Nikki was caulking. Nikki was reaching. High. Nikki's suit was reaching high, too. The leg had crept upward, exposing the pale curve of her hips.

Now, that was sexy. He'd admit it. He was a man. A man enjoyed sights like this. Even engaged—and married—men could enjoy them. And since he was both, he'd enjoy himself. Academically.

Academically, Nikki looked hot.

Lowering her arms, she inspected the caulking bead, absently hooking a thumb at the leg of her suit and tugging it into place.

Carter exhaled and leaned back in the chair, balancing it on two legs. That wasn't so bad, was it? He wasn't going to fall apart just because Nikki flashed a little thigh.

His gaze followed her hand as she brought it upward to tug at the back of her top. She shifted the caulking gun to that hand before reaching upward, smoothing the caulking bead. Then she tugged at the opposite side of her suit.

And tugged the fastener right out.

The back sprang open. Carter's muscles convulsed and his chair teetered over, sending him sprawling on the fly bridge.

"Carter?"

"What?"

"Are you okay?"

I might never father children. "Fine."

"What happened?"

"Chair fell over."

"I've told you not to tilt the chair like that," she scolded. "You probably gouged the deck."

He had. "Looks fine."

Carter lay on his back, mocked by the striped awning, until he could move without further injuring himself.

When he righted his chair, he saw that Nikki, top secure once more, had finished replacing the window frame and had moved to the next one. She was almost directly below him and if he chose, he could view the shadowy cleft between her breasts.

But if he looked at her, he knew what would happen. So he wouldn't look at her.

And it didn't matter.

All he could think about was how he would have been able to see a lot more than clefts, shadowy or not, had his chair not fallen over.

He hadn't been this aroused since he was eighteen. What was he going to have to do, pack himself in ice?

He might as well look.

HE WAS LOOKING at her. That must mean he still found her attractive.

Smiling to herself, Nikki unscrewed the frame of the perfect-fitting window and prepared to recaulk it. One couldn't be too diligent in tracking down leaks. Of course, if the window weren't located right below Carter, she wouldn't be destroying a perfectly tight seal.

She stopped for a moment and tugged at her suit. The elastic was shot and she knew it. She hadn't worn the uncomfortable suit in a couple of seasons and had only kept it for sentimental reasons.

Today, she was full of sentiment.

Wiping her forehead, she resumed her attack on the window. It was blisteringly hot and normally she'd save jobs such as this for the early morning or evening, but Carter was out here and she, sentimental female that she was, wanted to be nearby.

She heard a splash and a shout and saw Carter grab for one of the fishing rods.

He stood and played out the line, a delighted grin on his lips.

Nikki stopped digging at the old compound to watch the battle. The rod was bent in a high arch. Carter had hooked a big one.

With his attention on the fish, Nikki took the opportunity to stare at Carter. Her A Woman's Place is in the House—and in the Senate shirt was plastered to his torso, reminding her that she'd neglected to tell him other clothes were available.

The muscles in his arms bunched as he fought the fish, patiently letting out line, then reeling it in.

Carter was a strong, solid man, who worked with weights to maintain his strength. He eschewed the overly muscled look for solidity.

Watching the muscles work in his arms and chest, Nikki was reminded of how it felt to be encircled by those arms. Secure, protected and very female.

Sweat beaded between her breasts and she blew a stream of air downward. Gooseflesh rose on her arms. She shuddered, at once both hot and cold in the heat.

"Got him!" With a shout of triumph, Carter ripped the fish from the ocean, nearly losing it as it writhed in a last wild struggle.

Shading her eyes, Nikki watched as he captured the line and its wiggling prize.

"A red snapper." Carter, wearing his disreputable hat, grinned down at her. "Must weigh four or five pounds!"

Probably three or four. "Great, you just caught dinner."

He looked pleased with himself. Man the forager. Woman the nurturer.

Carter admired his fish a moment longer, then, pole and all, he climbed down from the fly bridge. "Have you got the live well set up?"

Nikki shook her head. "I didn't think to."

Carter looked around. "I'll have to use that bucket, then." Without warning, he thrust his fish and pole toward her.

"Ick." Nikki held the squirming fish away from her, feeling sorry for it. She'd never felt comfortable meeting her food before she ate it.

Carter lowered the bucket over the side, dipped it into the ocean and raised it. Motioning for Nikki to bring him the fish, he untied the line around the handle.

Nikki gladly relinquished the fish. As Carter removed the hook, the fish gave one last lurch and scooted from his hands straight toward Nikki, striking her with its cold sliminess. She shrieked and batted it away, instantly feeling idiotic. The fish slid and flopped across the varnished deck.

"It's going over the side!" Carter shouted.

They both lunged for the fish at the same time, neither getting a good hold on it.

The fish continued its slithery attempt at escape, with Nikki laughing so hard, she could barely crawl after it.

"That's our dinner!" Carter protested when she gave up and sat on the deck, laughing helplessly.

Scooping up the fish, he dumped it into the bucket, then dipped his hands in the salt water and dried them on the T-shirt she'd lent him.

"Oh, yuck, Carter!"

"What's wrong?"

"That's my favorite T-shirt. You're going to make it smell all fishy."

"Where else am I supposed to dry my hands?" He looked all around before a devious gleam entered his eyes. "Where, Nikki? On you?" Extending his arms, he advanced toward her.

"No!" She scooted backward until she bumped into the canister holding the emergency life raft.

Carter stood in front of her, blocking her escape.

Trapped.

"I've got fish scales on my fingers," he taunted.

"Car-ter!" Giggling, she inched to one side.

"And soon they'll be on you . . ." He trailed off with an evil laugh.

She ducked her head and held her arms out protectively. "I'm already slimy from when the fish attacked me."

Leaning down, Carter grabbed her by her arms and lifted her to her feet.

"Where?"

"Here." Nikki patted her throat and chest, encountering a stray fish scale. Peeling it off with her fingernail, she thrust it right in front of his face. "See?"

Carter moved her hand away from his face and squinted at her fingers. "*One* scale?"

"There are probably more," Nikki said defensively, looking down at herself.

"I don't see any more." Still holding her wrist, Carter brushed at her throat.

On the second stroke, he froze, then as if in slow motion, he curled his fingers away from her skin.

Nikki shivered and her skin tightened.

A hot breeze puffed over the gulf waters. A gull cried.

As their awareness of each other grew, the very air changed around them.

Nikki looked up and her gaze collided with Carter's.

Heat waves shimmered, not all of them caused by the afternoon sun beating down.

Neither moved.

Nikki found it hard to breathe. All the oxygen had been burnt out of the air.

After endless moments of looking into her eyes, Carter shifted his gaze to her mouth.

Nikki's lips parted. She'd melt if he kissed her. She'd melt if he didn't.

She swayed toward him at the exact moment he tugged on her wrist. As their lips met, she felt him shudder, then enfold her in his arms.

She'd come home.

She'd had no lovers since Carter, had desired no lovers since Carter. And now, locked in his arms, she knew she could never love anyone else.

Nikki drew her arms over his shoulders, standing on tiptoe to fit closer to him, just the way she always had. It was automatic, and she was never conscious of doing it. Only afterward would she become aware of the slight ache in the arches of her feet.

Carter's arms fit around her waist and his hands cupped her hips as he drew her closer to him.

He wanted her, she knew. And she wanted him. Knocking off his hat and burying her hands in his hair, she pressed herself closer in response, aided by the erotic pitching of the *Honey Bee*.

Carter's kiss was at once familiar, yet subtly different and Nikki was reminded that while she'd had no lovers, Carter had been about to marry Dee Ann.

A furious jealousy poured through her. She grabbed a handful of his hair. When he gasped, she plunged her tongue into his mouth, determined to obliterate all memory of Dee Ann Karrenbrock.

The vibrations of Carter's low moan pulsed from his mouth to hers, giving Nikki an elemental satisfaction.

Carter was hers.

Reveling in her power, she changed the tenor of their kiss, caressing rather than branding. Rewarding instead of punishing.

She was in control and with that control, Nikki found the freedom to be herself. Not Carter's employee, nor his wife, but the woman she wanted to be.

And the woman she wanted to be bit Carter Belden on the lip.

"Nikki!" Carter, his eyes glazed, stared at her, his expression a mixture of delighted shock.

"Yes, *Nikki*," she said, hooking her arms around his neck and drawing his head back to hers.

He resisted, so she stood back on her heels, using her weight as leverage.

"Nikki," he repeated, but differently this time. His hands slid down her shoulders and pulled at her arms.

She stood back on tiptoe, but he held himself away.

"Nikki," he said again, his voice flat.

At last sensing the change, she released him.

Carter's tongue wet his lips as if savoring a last taste of her, lingering along the slightly reddened lower one. "Nikki . . ." It was a sigh.

She made as if to kiss him again, but was stopped by the regretful shake of his head.

"We . . . can't."

"Oh, yes, we can," she said. "And we have. Many times."

"I remember." He closed his eyes.

She slid her arms around his waist. "Shall we refresh your memories?"

"No." He softened his refusal by resting his head on top of hers. "I feel as though I'm picking my way through a moral mine field. We may be married, but I'm engaged to someone else."

After a moment, Nikki said, "Do you realize what you just said?"

He winced. "I realize that I'm not going to sleep at all tonight."

"Carter, we—"

He touched a finger to her lips. "It wouldn't be right."

Angry, Nikki stepped away from him. "How can it *not* be right?" When he didn't answer, she lashed out at him, "You don't love Dee Ann!"

"Love wasn't part of my agreement with Dee Ann."

His admission didn't give Nikki the satisfaction she thought it would.

"But I do have a commitment to her," he continued gently.

"You have a commitment to me!"

"*Had*, Nikki."

At his pitying look, Nikki would have given anything to recall her words. "I see." Stepping back farther, she tucked a wisp of hair behind her ear. "Then I hope you and Dee Ann will be very happy together."

8

FOR THE FIRST TIME in his life, Carter couldn't concentrate on Belden Industries. A silent Nikki had produced a duffel bag containing his clothes, then had left him alone. He'd been holed up in the stateroom for three hours, but he hadn't managed to accomplish much, except to avoid her.

Emotionally, he felt as if the rug had been pulled out from under him. His hot desire for Nikki had caught him completely unaware. Had it been bubbling beneath the surface all these years waiting until now to erupt?

Even during their marriage, he hadn't felt such a burning need. *He* controlled his wants and desires—they didn't control him.

And why Nikki? Why not Dee Ann? He'd looked forward to a full and enjoyable life with Dee Ann—very similar to the one he'd had with Nikki, the main difference being that Dee Ann wouldn't spend her days working for him.

He suspected that this had contributed to his breakup with Nikki. Too much togetherness was bad for a marriage.

And children. Dee Ann wanted two and he agreed. It was time for children.

That *was* why men and women married, wasn't it? A man's children needed his name. A woman needed the legal protection. He understood the rules and was ready to abide by them.

Nikki was breaking the rules.

And tempting him to break them right along with her.

He checked the captain's wall clock and grimaced. It was almost eighteen hundred hours—six o'clock and time for the check-in. Sighing, he stared at the papers spread around him in a semicircle and tried to concentrate.

Once it had been pointed out to him, the pattern of stock trades was obvious.

Someone had gone to a great deal of trouble to hide the pattern and would have succeeded if Nikki and her crew hadn't questioned why Lacefield Foods would have the slightest interest in owning stock in a manufacturing supply company. Belden Industries didn't make small containers—they fabricated huge pieces of equipment. Karrenbrock must have assumed no one would notice.

And, Carter now dared to admit, Dee Ann and her mother had kept him so off-balance with their countless interruptions, he hadn't been as sharp as he should have been.

They couldn't have done it on purpose, could they?

For a moment, Carter considered that option. Why would Dee Ann agree to such a plot? What would she gain by sabotaging her future husband's company? Besides, she'd never indicated the slightest interest in the workings of Belden Industries. Dee Ann desired a certain type of life and Carter was prepared to support her. In return, he would no longer have to worry about his domestic and social responsibilities.

No. Actively participating on the board of directors would be contrary to Dee Ann's goals. If he lost control of their source of income, that would also be contrary to her goals because he'd risk everything to start over again. Therefore, he should tell Julian—no, Saunders—to contact Dee Ann with a message from him. Carter wasn't terribly concerned about the exact wording of the message. He'd tell her that Belden Industries needed his full attention right now. She'd still be angry, but she was a businessman's daughter. She'd understand.

Satisfied with his conclusions, Carter gathered the papers and prepared to hear the six o'clock report.

And then he was going to clean a fish.

"CARTER, the fish escaped!" Breathless, Nikki appeared in the doorway of the galley. When she saw what he was doing, her jaw dropped. "You're cleaning the fish!"

He tossed a glance at her. "And I intend to cook it, too."

Nikki stared at the unfamiliar sight of Carter in the galley.

"In fact," he said as he opened the tiny refrigerator, "I'm going to cook the entire dinner." He withdrew a bottle of white wine and uncorked it.

"Where did you get that?" Nikki asked, seeing the label. She knew she didn't have wine of that caliber on board.

Carter poured her a glass. "I found two bottles in the duffel bag with my clothes. Julian must have raided my wine rack when he packed."

Nikki accepted the glass with a grin. "Julian does know his wines."

"That he does." A corner of Carter's mouth quirked upward. "Now go sit on deck and relax. I'll bring you dinner."

She sipped the wine, savoring its cool crispness. It was exactly the sort of wine one could drink too much of if one wasn't careful. "Cooking didn't used to be among your talents."

Carter eyed the fish. "And it still isn't, but I'm hoping that after a couple of glasses of wine, you won't notice."

Nikki laughed. "I'm going to check on things in the pilothouse and then I'll come back down here and watch you."

"So you can feel superior?"

Nikki pushed herself away from the door. "No, because I find the sight of a man in the kitchen incredibly sexy."

Chew on that, Mr. I'm-committed-to-Dee Ann.

Carter was cooking for her. What a novelty. Not once during their entire marriage had he ever cooked for her. Instantly, she wondered if this was Dee Ann's influence, then banished the thought. So what if it was?

Nikki punched the knob on the weather radio. She hadn't had a chance to check the instruments earlier, when she and Carter had listened to Saunders's report.

He, Julian and Bob had rented a beach house within walking distance of Nikki's dock. They'd spent the day calling stockholders and researching trades within the last ninety days. They'd learned nothing new, except that someone had been contacting major shareholders before they had.

Nikki wasn't surprised, but Carter took it as a personal betrayal that some shareholders had sold out. The company bore his name; it was unthinkable that he wouldn't run it.

They discussed possible countermaneuvers, but until trading began tomorrow, Monday, there wasn't anything concrete to do.

Nikki had experienced a bad moment when Carter dictated a message for Saunders to give to Dee Ann, but then conceded that his loyalty to her was appropriate.

Misplaced, but appropriate.

Nikki stretched, and sipped her wine, watching the sunset from the pilothouse. No storms, no incipient hurricanes. They were still firmly anchored and had plenty of supplies.

And they were alone.

It was a setting for romance.

Too bad Carter didn't want to take advantage of it.

Too bad that she wanted him to.

Leaving the pilothouse, Nikki stepped onto the deck. Now that evening had lessened the intensity of the sun's rays, cooling breezes swept over the water and fluttered the white gauzy pants and tunic she'd changed into earlier. It was as if the gulf had held its breath all day long and now exhaled.

She stood at the railing and sipped the last of her wine, feeling as if she was at the brink of something important. No doubt it was just the waiting. The Belden Industries team could do nothing until tomorrow. For now, there was only the waiting.

For now, there was only Carter and Nikki.

CARTER POURED himself a glass of wine, then added a splash into the pan with the fish. "I figure we could both use some," he muttered to the fillets.

The fillets hissed in response and Carter turned down the heat. Obviously, too hot.

"Smells wonderful," said a soft voice behind him.

Nikki propped a portable radio behind the retaining bar on the shelf above the table.

"That looks like a new toy," Carter commented.

"It is. I don't want to be out of contact when I'm sailing the *Honey Bee* by myself," she explained. "If Julian or Saunders wants to reach us, they can."

"I remember a time when we didn't want to be contacted," Carter murmured.

She set her empty wineglass on the dinette table. "Times have changed." There was an edge to her voice that was in contrast with the flimsy thing she was wearing.

She was entitled. He shouldn't make suggestive comments when he didn't intend to act on them.

He eased the fillets over. They only stuck a little and landed mostly in one piece. Not pretty, but they should taste good.

"Another couple of minutes and we can eat," he said. Withdrawing the wine from the refrigerator, he refilled her glass, then looked up to tell her he'd done so.

The words died on his lips. Nikki, hugging her arms around herself, stood at the salon windows, drenched in the light of the setting sun. Carter could clearly see the outline of her slim body through her clothes.

As he watched, she fluffed at the back of her hair. It was much shorter than she'd worn it during their marriage. He'd barely noticed when she'd cut it. As a rule, short hair on women didn't appeal to him, but he was breaking all sorts of rules this weekend.

The top she wore was cut like a man's undershirt and the scooped back revealed the lines of her neck. He couldn't remember noticing Nikki's neck before. It seemed like an odd thing to notice now.

Her fingers brushed at her hair again and he could see that the short ends were tangling the two gold chains she wore.

The glinting drew him and before he knew it, he'd abandoned the wine and the fish and was walking across the salon. "Let me."

Startled, she swiveled her head, but his fingers were separating the chains.

Her skin was smooth and soft.

He wanted to taste it.

He bent his head.

"The fish!" Nikki ran toward the galley where his efforts at dinner were stinking up the cabin.

Grabbing the pan from the stove, she climbed the steps to the deck, leaving Carter staring after her.

He hesitated a moment, then with a shrug, grabbed her wine and his and followed.

She stood by the railing, staring at the pan's contents.

"Shall we toss it over the side?" he asked.

"Oh, no." Nikki smiled up at him. "Only the bottom is scorched. We'll just peel off the fish and leave that layer in the pan."

"Then would you like to trade?" He indicated her wine.

With a bit of awkward maneuvering, Nikki ended up with her wine and Carter held the pan of fish. "Let's eat out here," he said, inspired by the cooling breezes and the orange sunset.

"Okay," Nikki agreed and started below.

"No. You sit here . . ." Using his feet, since his hands were full, Carter tried to pull out a lounge chair without spilling either the fish or his wine. "I'll bring up everything."

She gave him a nod of acknowledgment and arranged herself on a nest of pillows, like a pasha's concubine. Taking a small sip of wine, she savored it, then smiled.

Carter looked around for somewhere to set down the frying pan.

Nikki held out her arms.

Her eyes glowed in the saffron light. Her lips, moistened by the wine, gleamed. What an invitation. Carter nearly took her up on it before he realized that he was supposed to hand her the fish.

This fish had been a lot of trouble, he thought as he spoiled her elegant pose by handing her a frying pan.

What happened to all your cool moves, Belden? Gone from lack of practice, no doubt.

Once below deck, he raced around, looking for a tray. Didn't they used to have a tray? How had Nikki managed to carry everything?

He couldn't find a tray and the thought of Nikki patiently sitting on deck with a pan of half-burned fish made him clumsy in his haste.

He stopped and drew a long, deep breath. *Calm down.* This was Nikki.

Nikki.

He closed his eyes. Nikki.

He was in trouble.

And he didn't care.

Putting the silverware in his pockets, Carter managed to juggle plates, a bowl of salad, Julian's leftover sourdough bread and the rest of the wine. When he emerged on deck, he discovered Nikki dragging both chairs closer to the railing.

Seeing him, she stood and walked toward him as the breeze molded her clothes to her body.

Carter froze. Or most of him did, anyway.

Nikki took the plates and the bread, leaving him with the salad, the wine bottle and the rather startling evidence of his desire.

"This will be nice," she said, bending over to retrieve the fish.

Between the breeze, the loose cut of her tank top and gravity, the fabric fell away from her bodice.

Carter looked. He couldn't help it. He felt like an eighteen-year-old with raging hormones.

Lucky for Nikki, she was wearing a bra, or she'd have found herself hauled down to the master stateroom.

Somehow, Carter managed to walk across the deck and ease himself into the chair. "Let me serve you," he said, trying to regain control.

Flashing him a smile, she settled in the chair expectantly and Carter managed a credible showing, though he hoped he never had to make a living as a waiter.

The fish was fine. The salad was fine. The bread was still fine.

The wine was the nectar of the gods, which was probably why everything seemed all golden and wonderful.

"So, what's your plan for tomorrow?" Nikki asked.

"Hmm?"

"To buy more Belden stock," she said with a smile.

Was her smile a knowing one? Did she have any idea that he'd abandoned all moral thought where she was concerned?

"I don't want to talk business," he said.

Nikki no longer smiled. *"What* did you say?"

"Tonight, no business talk. I'm dining with a beautiful woman and I want to talk about her."

She stilled. "Who?"

"You, Nikki," he told her, irritated. She looked so flabbergasted.

"What about me?"

Now she looked suspicious and that hurt his pride. Was it so unusual for him to flirt with her?

Yes, he supposed it was. They'd never had a flirting kind of relationship. Their relationship had been more the explosive kind. And it had exploded right after they'd worked for sixty hours straight on a presentation for a meeting at the Hotel Galvez.

When Belden Industries' bid had been accepted, there had been a lot of backslapping and handshaking. And hugging and kissing. Lots of kissing.

And then there was the celebratory champagne in the Belden Industries hospitality suite.

And more kissing.

By that time, he'd narrowed the kissing down to pretty much one person.

Nikki.

She was so smart and clever and loyal and enthusiastic. And she'd had a bit of a crush on him. He knew it and under the guise of happiness and champagne, he'd thought a couple kisses wouldn't matter.

They'd gone to bed that night and hadn't come out for three days.

Two weeks later, they were married.

"Carter? What are you thinking?"

"About the first time we slept together," he answered, without considering the effect of his words.

Her silence told him he should have thought more. "The way you look...your outfit...the white...reminds me of our wedding."

Her eyes darkened, but he couldn't tell what she was thinking. "I wore a white sarong and a lei," she murmured, looking down at herself.

"Must be the white."

Nikki gave him a funny look. "You're sure in a weird mood."

"I was just waxing nostalgic," he replied, stung.

"Is this the same man who said, 'Looking back means you won't see problems until you run into them'?"

"I appear to have run into them, anyway."

"Mmm." She continued to eye him thoughtfully. "What went wrong, Nikki?"

There were several ways she could have answered his question, but Nikki seemed to sense he was referring to their marriage. "I don't think we were ever really married," she said slowly.

"That goes with not ever really being divorced," was his glib comment.

She linked her fingers around the wine goblet. "You're used to making things happen, Carter. You don't like to get stale, so you make decisions quickly and you never look back. But some things take time to develop." She held up the glass. "Wine, for example. Good barbecue. Lasting relationships."

"But we've known each other for years," he protested.

"Have we?"

A trick question. He was being maneuvered into a trap, but it was a trap of his own making. "Before this weekend, I *thought* so."

Nikki shook her head. "You only knew a part of me, but it was my own fault. That's all I ever showed you."

"Are you saying you have a dark side?"

"A different side." She raised an eyebrow. "Maybe more sides."

"Why *didn't* you show them to me?"

"I suppose I thought you wouldn't be interested," she said with a shrug.

"That was presumptuous of you."

"Maybe. Maybe not."

Carter didn't like the way the conversation was going. Although he'd started it, he found he didn't want to know what had gone wrong. It had and it was over, period.

"Think about our wedding," Nikki instructed him.

Carter didn't want to think about it anymore.

"On the beach at sunset," Nikki continued. "White flowers, torches, surrounded by family."

"Wait a minute . . . I'm the guy who grew up in foster homes. I don't have any family."

"Yes, you do. Belden Industries is your family."

Carter was struck by the sudden truth of her remark. "I'd never thought about it that way, but I guess you're right."

"I, however, do have family. You met my parents at the wedding, remember?"

"Of course." But he couldn't drag a mental picture of them out of his memory. Ashamed, he looked away.

"They barely made it. Buying airline tickets at the last minute was very expensive for them. My sister didn't even get to come. She was really hurt, you know."

"I'd forgotten that." Forgotten that she even had a sister. "We could have postponed the wedding a couple of weeks. Why didn't you say something?"

Nikki shook her head, a wistful expression on her face. "I was afraid you'd change your mind about marrying me."

"Ah, Nikki." Carter felt like a heel. It was true, once he decided on a plan of action, he loathed wasting time.

Which made it all the more incredible that Dee Ann and her mother had been able to persuade him to agree to yesterday's dog-and-pony show. But even that had been rushed. He'd overheard countless remarks marveling at how quickly everything had been planned.

He stared down at his wine, took a sip—took the time to savor it—and gazed out at the last of the sunset. It wasn't so very different from the sunset the evening he'd married Nikki. Glancing back at her, he found her silently watching him, one leg tucked underneath her.

As his gaze tangled with hers, she reached out and drew her knuckles across his cheek and jaw. "Like I said, I made mistakes."

Carter captured her hand, placed a kiss in the center of the palm, then closed her fingers over it. "The difference is that you noticed. I didn't."

She nodded, then changed the subject. "I'd better get these washed."

"Let's make it a joint venture," he offered, taking the pan and standing.

"But you cooked."

Carter grinned. "A gross exaggeration, but thanks, anyway."

Laughing companionably, they descended to the galley.

Their camaraderie extended until the last plate was secured in the cabinet.

It was the most natural thing in the world to return to the salon. Nikki curled onto one of the banquettes and Carter sat on the corner of the other.

She was a good listener and Carter found himself talking, of all things, about his childhood in foster homes. He'd never confided much to anyone before. There wasn't much to confide. He hadn't been mistreated, but the longest he'd lived with any one family had been eighteen months.

"That's probably why you like to do everything so quickly," Nikki commented. "You never knew when things were going to change."

"Maybe. So. What was your childhood like?"

Nikki painted what she thought was a typical American childhood from watermelon on the Fourth of July to Girl Scouts to proms and college.

She thought it was typical. To Carter, it was as exotic as the customs of a foreign people. He drank it all in and wondered why they'd never talked like this before.

What else had he missed?

He watched as she punctuated her sentences with graceful hand movements that flashed the gold bangle she wore. When her head moved, her matching earrings swung and caught the light.

She wore no lipstick, yet her lips were the exact shade of the inside of a conch shell.

The more they talked, the more he wanted her and the more he wanted her eyes to light with desire for him.

They talked so long, their mouths became dry, so they finished off the bottle of wine. Then they talked some more.

It was late enough so they could go to bed, but not so late that they should. And Carter didn't want the evening to end. Watching Nikki move around the salon, stretching her stiff muscles, was sweet torture.

How could he have let her go?

Why hadn't he recognized what he had when they were together?

She yawned and he was afraid she'd tell him she was on her way to bed.

"So . . . how about some cards? We've never played cards together, have we, Nikki?"

"Not that I can remember." She hesitated and he held his breath. Walking to a cabinet, she opened it and dug inside, unearthing a pack of cards.

Carter exhaled.

"Do you want to play Hearts?" she asked, sitting at the dinette table.

"I don't know how."

"I could teach you—or how about gin rummy?"

His childhood was more deprived than he thought.

Nikki opened the pack and riffled through the cards. "Poker?"

Now *that* was a game he knew how to play. "What kind? Five-card stud? Seven-card draw? Highball? Lowball? Deuces and one-eyed jacks wild?"

Shaking her head, Nikki shuffled the cards.

"What, then?"

She slapped the cards on the table and leaned forward on her elbows. "Strip."

9

"WHAT?"

"Strip poker." Nikki's smile bordered on a leer. She'd never played strip poker before. Suggesting it now was very naughty of her. Look how nervous the idea made Carter.

And rightly so. Nikki'd had it. Actually, she *hadn't* had it, but wanted it. And she wanted it soon. Carter had been devouring her with his eyes for the last hour and she wanted to call his bluff, so to speak. He couldn't look at her that way without expecting her to respond.

"Very funny," Carter said without laughing. "Now, where are the chips?"

"Don't have any. That's why I think strip poker is such a great idea."

"We can use toothpicks." Carter practically ran to search the galley.

"There aren't any toothpicks either."

"Beans."

"Nope."

"Pretzels?" Carter sounded desperate.

"Come here, Carter." Nikki crooked her finger. The more he protested, the more daring she felt.

"I don't think so."

"Why not?"

"It's not a good idea."

"I think it's a splendid idea." She began shuffling the cards.

Carter's reluctance excited her. There was the element of the forbidden. Morally, Nikki supposed she was the "other woman." Morally, not technically. And there was something deliciously wicked about being the "other woman."

She looked at him from under her lashes. He stood a few feet away, his lips parted, a look of intense longing on his face. Had he ever looked at her that way before? No, because he usually got what he wanted before he even knew he wanted it.

Not this time.

She shivered with anticipation. Oh, she was going to enjoy being a wicked woman. This was a facet of her personality that even *she* hadn't known about.

She wished she were wearing less clothes. But that could be arranged, if she played her cards right.

Nikki squared the deck and set it in the middle of the table. Looking up at Carter, who was the most appealing example of conflicting emotions she'd ever seen, she gestured to the cards. "Cut?"

Like an old man, Carter moved stiffly to the table. He stared down at the cards. "I—do you know how to play poker?"

"Sure," she said with breezy confidence.

Carter nodded once, then cut the cards.

"Just not very well," she added.

His eyes widened. "So you might lose."

Nikki began to shuffle. "Depends on your definition of losing."

HE SHOULD NEVER have agreed to this, Carter thought as sweat beaded on his forehead. He thought she was kidding. He thought she'd chicken out. *Don't look at your hand. Once you look at your hand, you're committed to the game.*

"You might be a better player, but I'm wearing more than you are, so that evens things up, don't you think?" Nikki asked as she started dealing the cards.

Carter couldn't think.

"Five? Seven?"

He stared at the pool of cards in front of him. "Seven." It would give her a better chance at getting a good hand. "Deuces and one-eyed jacks wild," he added.

"Oooh." She gave an unNikki-like giggle. "I like the sound of wild."

"Nikki?" He peered at her. "Are you drunk?"

Her laughter rippled. "On half a bottle of wine over four hours?"

That's it. Offer more wine. Get her drunk. She'd pass out and his problem would be solved.

Unless she passed out before he got to see her naked.

Where had that thought come from? What was the matter with him? Had he abandoned all loyalty to what's-her-name?

He leapt from the table. "I'm going to open the other bottle of wine," he declared.

"Sounds *delicious*," she said, crinkling her nose.

Carter poured each of them a fresh glass of wine, drank half of his, then refilled it. It was a shame to guzzle this wine, but these were desperate times. *You're supposed to be getting her drunk.* Right.

"A toast," he said and handed her the glass.

"To?"

"To . . . good hands."

"Car-ter." She drew out his name. "You already have good hands."

Carter cleared his throat. "To friends," he amended firmly.

"To friends with good hands," Nikki said, clinking her glass on his.

Carter's hands tingled as he looked at the cards she'd dealt him. "Did you shuffle these cards?" he demanded.

Nikki blinked innocently. "Why, Carter, you cut the deck."

He had three of a kind, even without using the wild card he'd been dealt. Four of a kind.

If he had any luck at all, Nikki would have five of a kind or six or . . .

"We have to ante up." She looked positively delighted.

"Uh . . ."

"How about our pants?"

"Nikki!"

"You're no fun," she said, pouting as she pulled off a hoop earring.

Scowling, Carter unstrapped his watch.

"What do you have?" she asked, trying to peek at his cards.

He held them close. "Now wait a minute. You have to pay to see these cards . . ." Carter's voice trailed off as Nikki eagerly began removing jewelry. "Stop. New rules. No antes. We'll just show our hands. Loser antes."

"Okay." Nikki pushed her bangle back on her wrist and flipped over her cards.

She had two pairs. Reluctantly, Carter turned over his own cards. "Four of a kind."

"I only see three," Nikki said.

"The jack is wild."

"I have a jack, why isn't he wild?"

"Because he has two eyes."

"I guess your jack lived dangerously."

Carter drew a deep breath. "You still want to play?"

"Of course!"

Scraping his winnings toward him, Carter gathered the cards. Nikki sat across from him expectantly, her right earlobe bare.

His deal. Each time he looked up at her, his eyes were drawn to her naked earlobe. It was amazing to him that an earring could make such a difference.

It was amazing to him that he was turned on by an earlobe.

"Do the wild cards have to match something, or can they be whatever you want?" She rubbed her ear absently.

"Whatever you want," he answered, hoping that she would have a better hand this time. How would he react to two naked earlobes?

"How lucky," she said, picking five cards from her seven and rearranging them.

Carter studied his options. He could use the wild card two as a seven and manage a straight. Or, he had a handful of clubs, thus making a flush. A flush was higher than a straight.

He tried to read Nikki's face, but she wore an enigmatically serene expression. A perfect poker face.

He made his selection and pushed the earring toward the center. "I've got a straight," he announced and leaned back so she could take back her earring.

"Two little pairs," she said and thrust out her lower lip.

"What?" Carter stared at her cards. "No. Add your jack to the fours and you'll have three of a kind."

"You said a wild card could be whatever I wanted."

"But three of a kind beats two pairs!"

"Does it beat a straight?"

Carter gazed into her seemingly guileless eyes. "No."

"So I lose, anyway." She rolled her bangle across the table. It bumped into his watch and fell to its side with a clatter.

"I can't believe you couldn't make a better hand than that," he said, reaching for the two discards.

"Well, let's see what you could have done," she said, reaching for his. "My, my. Look at all these clubs. What's it called when you have a whole handful of one thing?"

Carter felt a tightening in the pit of his stomach. "A flush."

"And it's less than a straight? I always get them confused."

Carter forced a smile as he gathered the cards. "It's easy to do. I, ah, have a little trouble myself. A flush is, in fact, higher than a straight."

"That's what I thought."

He was able to demonstrate this on the very next hand when his heart flush won over Nikki's straight. Her other earring joined its mate.

Soon Carter had added one necklace and a deck shoe to his winnings.

He'd never had such a run of luck—but he wasn't certain if this was bad luck or good luck.

To his utter mortification, his hands trembled as he squared the cards for the deal. To cover his nervousness, he sipped his wine, noting that Nikki did, as well. Their eyes met over the rims of their glasses. Hers were clear and knowing.

She was not anywhere near becoming drunk and she knew exactly what she was doing.

Why was he letting her?

Carter's heart had kicked into high gear from the first deal. His shirt was drenched. He felt both hot and cold.

Dealing quickly to mask his agitation, Carter decided to leave everything in fate's hands.

Fate dealt him a full house.

Fate dealt Nikki three of a kind.

Carter added her other shoe to his winnings.

He drained his wine. It might as well have been water. He felt sharply alive. His mind raced. His heart pounded. An ache throbbed persistently in his groin. A lone gold chain was all the jewelry she wore.

Nikki's fingers curled around her wineglass.

Carter watched in fascination as she slowly took a sip and swallowed, then flicked her tongue to moisten her lips.

It was her deal.

HIS EYES were scorching her. Nikki could feel the heat rising from her skin, could feel her body respond as if he'd touched her.

The air was heavy with tension. The lighthearted mood in which she'd started the game had turned serious.

Sounds were magnified. Her breathing. Carter's breathing. The slap of the cards and the pounding of her heart.

Her throat was dry and she drank more wine, inhaling its fragrance with heightened appreciation.

One by one, she dealt the cards in silence. When she finished, they both stared at them.

Before she picked up her cards, she met Carter's hypnotizing gaze.

He wanted her and she was going to make him admit it. It wouldn't be easy. Knowing Carter, he was looking at this game as a test of his self-control, a test he always passed.

Just once, Nikki wanted to see him fail.

Breathing shallowly, she picked up her cards and saw a full house almost immediately.

Disappointment knifed through her. She could only win by losing and a full house was a good hand.

Carter had barely looked at his cards and now watched her, his expression resigned.

Well, she couldn't expect to lose every hand, Nikki thought and lay down her full house.

Carter's gaze never left her as he fanned out his cards.

Four kings and a wild card. Five kings.

He'd won the round.

Fate was on her side.

Nikki touched her gold chain, but didn't want to tempt fate after it had given her this opportunity to up the ante.

Slowly, she stood, then crossed her arms and grasped the hem of her tunic. In one fluid movement, she pulled it over her head, then dangled it in front of Carter. "Your winnings, sir."

He seemed frozen.

Nikki released the tunic and it rippled into a gauzy pool, spilling from the table to his lap.

She stood before him as his gaze traveled over her.

"You never used to wear underwear like that," he said, his voice unrecognizable.

No, she hadn't. But Carter's announcement of his engagement to the couture-clad Dee Ann was a blow to Nikki's sense of feminine attractiveness. In one impulsive shopping spree, she'd replaced all her sensible cottons with lingerie that emphasized allure over function.

Only afterward did she acknowledge that no one was likely to see her in them, but that hadn't been the point. The point had been to reassure herself that she was an appealing, sensual woman, even though Carter was unaware of it.

Now, of course, she was making him aware of it.

Nikki inhaled. Her breasts, encased in exquisitely worked apricot lace and silk, tightened. The lingerie had been wildly, wickedly and wantonly expensive.

And, judging by the hot desire burning in Carter's hazel eyes, worth every penny.

She slid onto the banquette and sipped her wine, aware that he followed her every movement.

Leaning back, she crossed her legs and propped her elbow on the shelf. "Your deal."

Silently, Carter gathered the cards, shuffled quickly and dealt.

As each card hit the table, Nikki's breath quickened. The cooling air from the vent whispered over her heated skin.

How could Carter stand this? Didn't he want to touch her as much as she wanted to be touched?

Forcing herself to keep her movements slow and languid, she picked up her cards with deliberate casualness. Glancing at Carter, she tried to read his expression even before studying her cards.

She learned nothing, except that he still held an iron grip on his self-control. Granted, that grip was shaking a little.

Nikki was not so disciplined. She held her cards low, making sure he could still see her delicately sheer bra.

Carter reached for his wine and Nikki smiled.

Then she saw her cards. A straight flush in diamonds. In this case, diamonds definitely weren't a girl's best friend. Carter could only beat her if he held five of a kind again.

Trying to hide her disappointment, Nikki fanned out her cards.

Carter had a straight.

Her breasts ached at the sight. Revealing herself in her provocative underwear had intensified Nikki's awareness of her body. She was surfing on a wave of sensuality and she wanted the ride to continue.

Carter's fingers dived into the tunic and Nikki resigned herself to slipping it back on. But instead of tossing it to her, he merely moved it to one side and extracted her necklace from the pile of his winnings.

Suspending it from one finger, he offered it to her.

Nikki raised an eyebrow.

"I like the look of gold next to your skin." The deep murmur of Carter's voice thrummed in the silence.

Nikki looked down at herself and saw the remaining necklace she wore follow the curves of her breasts and dip into the hollow between them. With a smile, she accepted and refastened the second necklace.

Play had progressed to a new, more intense, level.

It had long since grown dark, but Nikki and Carter relied on the small table light, which left the rest of the salon shadowed.

She won the following round and her bangle back.

When her next hand contained a full house, Nikki fully expected to regain one of her earrings.

"Four aces," Carter said, lying down one ace and, appropriately, three wild cards.

He'd won. Nikki's heart thudded. *I like the look of gold next to your skin.* She toyed with the bangle. It glimmered in the muted light.

Leaning back, Carter watched the movements of her fingers with a heavy-lidded gaze.

I like the look of gold next to your skin.

Stroking her arm, Nikki slowly pushed the bangle up on her wrist. Watching Carter watch her, she trailed her fingers along her arm and across her collarbone, entwining the chains.

Carter seemed hypnotized as she plucked first at one chain, then the other, teasing and taunting him.

. . . gold next to your skin . . . next to your skin.

Did he speak or were those echoes conjured by her mind in its erotic trance?

Nikki surrendered to the seduction of the gentle movement of the cabin and Carter's fascination with her hands. He held his breath as she raised her elbows and drew her hands behind her head. He exhaled as she stopped. But Nikki arched her back in a feline stretch and Carter's eyes widened once more.

Feeling powerful and in control, she stood. Skimming her hands down her rib cage, Nikki trifled with the drawstring on her pants.

Carter's breathing slowed.

. . . gold on skin . . .

Nikki took a step toward him. Then another.

Carter swallowed.

Deliberately, Nikki raised her fingers to the front hook of her bra.

Held rigidly to his sides, Carter's hand's tightened into fists.

With the slightest of tugs, Nikki unclasped the hook. Holding the ends of lace together, she savored Carter's immediate reaction.

From the betraying bulge in his pants to his parted lips, she could see that he was completely and totally in her power. For the first time ever, Nikki knew she had Carter's sheer and undivided attention. She consumed his every thought. Not Belden Industries and not Dee Ann Karrenbrock.

She celebrated her victory by separating the cups just enough so the straps loosened and whispered down her arms. Nikki was so focused on Carter's reaction, she was surprised by her own jolt of desire as the lace fell to her elbows.

Carter had never looked at her the way he was looking at her now—as a lover, in every sense of the word. And Nikki had never felt the confidence to appear before him as she did now—demanding and in control. Reveling in her own awakened sensuality.

His gaze met hers with a hint of a dare. Did he think she wouldn't? Couldn't?

Nikki looked him right in the eye, then, opening the bra as if she were opening her heart, she bared her breasts.

Carter inhaled through parted lips. It wasn't quite a gasp, but it wasn't normal breathing, either. "You look like a pagan goddess," he managed to say, his voice rough.

"Wait till you see my altar," she murmured. Leaning close, she dropped the bra on top of the tunic, then sat at her place.

She felt free. She felt sexy. She felt like a loose woman.

"I . . . can't remember whose deal it is," Carter said.

"I'LL DEAL," said the pagan goddess.

Which was a good thing since Carter didn't trust himself to handle the cards. Not when he wanted to be handling other things.

He'd always known Nikki was attractive, but there was a world of difference between attractive and the stunningly beautiful woman sitting across from him.

Who had taught her such self-confidence? he wondered with an unreasonable surge of jealousy. She knew how to arouse him to an unbearable peak and he was powerless against her. This game had become a contest of wills he was no longer certain he'd win.

The golden gleam of her necklaces caught his eye as she dealt. He wanted to cover her in gold chains and see her wearing them just as she was now—with nothing else.

One earring rolled back and forth across the table until at last, Carter won two hands in a row.

Nikki stood and Carter wanted to take her in his arms and carry her off to the master stateroom, but the determined look in her eyes stopped him. She wanted something from him, something other than a nostalgic trip to bed.

At this point, if he had any idea what it was, he'd give it to her. He'd give her anything. Anything to end this intolerable tension.

Nikki's hands skimmed her body before pulling at the gold-tipped cords that fastened the waistband of her pants.

Gently tugging, she untied them, loosened the gathers and the white trousers were history.

All she wore were satin and lace thong bikinis.

A guttural sound escaped him. He heard it, but was powerless to prevent it.

Nikki heard it, too, the self-satisfied look on her face told him as much. She stepped out of her pants, hooked them with her foot and extended one of her mile-long legs toward him.

Carter pulled the fabric out of the way, grasping her calf when she tried to withdraw it. His action caught her off guard and she grabbed the back of the bench to maintain her balance.

Carter inhaled the light breezy scent she wore as he stroked her calf and foot. He couldn't let her go, not before he tasted her once more.

Bending down, he kissed the arch of her foot, pleased by her soft gasp. He moved to her ankle, pressing kisses along her calf as far as he could reach. Just below her knee, he scooted forward, pulling her closer.

She pulled back and, dazed, he looked up.

"Tell me that you want me," she instructed him.

"I want you."

"Mean it."

"I *want* you."

"Try again."

And then he understood. "I want *you*. Only you."

"Yes."

And she was in his arms, kissing him with wild abandon.

Carter buried his hand in her hair and ran the other up her thigh to the hip left bare by the bikinis. He settled her firmly in his lap, leaving her in no doubt of his desire.

He could hear the blood pounding in his ears and wondered if he were going to explode. His heart raced and when he dropped kisses across her throat, he could feel Nikki's race, as well.

"Nikki . . . we've got . . . to move . . ."

She groaned and wiggled her way off his lap, turning to unzip his shorts.

He gasped and she giggled.

And the radio burped.

Two more static bursts followed. Nikki patted him. "Hold that thought," she said, stretching over to turn off the radio.

"...Carter...there—" came through the speaker just before she turned the knob.

"What was that?" Carter asked.

"Sounded like Julian. Stand up."

He did and Nikki nearly ripped off his shirt. "But, shouldn't we—"

She stopped him with a breath-stealing kiss and for a moment all he could think about was the feel of her breasts crushed against his chest.

Then the radio intruded.

"Nikki," he began.

She ripped her mouth from his. *"Damn!"* She held her head for an instant, then roughly jerked at the radio knob.

"...Ni-kkeeeeeee..."

"What?" she snarled into the microphone.

"Did I wake you?" Julian asked. "It's only ten o'clock. I thought there was a chance you'd be in the pilothouse."

She took two deep breaths before responding. "What's up?"

"Is Carter there?"

Carter zipped up his shorts. Nikki jerked her head toward him at the sound, then, looking resigned, handed him the microphone.

"I'm here, Julian."

"Sorry to bother you—" Carter didn't think he sounded all that sorry "—but Saunders just got back from the office. A courier delivered a package from Dee Ann this afternoon."

"Is it a bomb?"

"It's not ticking."

"Did you open it?"

"Saunders informed me that federal law prohibited me from opening mail addressed to another person."

"Saunders is a wimp. Anyway, you said a courier delivered it."

"I resent that, Carter," Saunders said. "Do we have your permission to open it?"

Carter sighed. They obviously thought it was important, or they wouldn't have tried to contact him. "Okay."

There was silence, during which Carter couldn't look at Nikki. He heard a rustling and figured she was dressing. He felt like a jerk. What could he say to her?

Nothing.

"Carter?" Saunders was still on the microphone. "It's, uh, it appears to be her engagement ring."

Carter felt an enormous burden lift from his shoulders. He was free. This time, he did look at Nikki.

She was wearing his shirt.

"The—well, there's no easy way to say this—the diamond has been pried out. Sorry."

If the price of a diamond was all it would cost him to extricate himself from this mess, Carter would pay it gladly. "Is there a note?"

"Yes."

"Read it."

"Are you sure?" Saunders obviously found the entire situation terribly uncomfortable.

"Read it."

Silence. Was it that horrible? What was Dee Ann threatening? To sue him, probably.

It was Julian's voice he heard next. "The message says, 'Carter. Rather than file a breach-of-contract suit, I'm keeping the diamond for future security.'"

"And that statement ought to hold up in court in case she changes her mind," Carter heard Saunders yell in the background.

"The odd thing is," Julian continued, "'future security' is capitalized. Why?"

Carter met Nikki's gaze. She shrugged and turned away.

"Don't go, Nikki."

"I'm tired."

"You weren't a few minutes ago."

"That was a few minutes ago."

"Come here."

She obviously didn't want to, but walked toward him. As soon as she was within reach, he seized the shirt and pulled it over her head. "That's better. I like the look of gold next to your skin."

"Carter? Does 'future security' have any special meaning to you?" Julian asked.

Carter grabbed Nikki with one hand and the microphone with the other. "No. And I'm not worrying about it tonight," he said, to both of them at the same time.

Nikki's face was luminous as she linked her arms around his neck.

"But we've got to be prepared for tomorrow," Julian protested.

"So go to bed." Carter drew his hand down the silky smoothness of her back. "I am."

10

SHE'D WON. Nikki could hardly believe it, but there was Carter, turning off the radio.

"See? Sometimes interruptions are worthwhile." He wrapped his arms around her and lowered his head. "I come to you a free man."

Just before he kissed her, Nikki asked, "Aren't you curious about what Dee Ann meant?"

"No," Carter said emphatically and lifted her off her feet. "And in a few moments, you won't be, either."

His kiss rattled her senses and she barely remembered him carrying her to the master stateroom. He set her on the bunk, murmuring as he kissed, of all things, her earlobe. "You have the sexiest ears."

"You're an ear man? Is *that* where I've gone wrong?"

"I didn't remember your ears. Your hair was always covering them."

"I'll keep it short," Nikki vowed as she redirected his mouth to hers.

She felt the warmth of Carter's hand as he caressed her from thigh to hip, then pulled at the edge of lace.

"Isn't this uncomfortable?" he breathed.

"Yes, oh, yes. Terribly uncomfortable."

"Then we'll just take it off," he said, doing so.

"What about you? Aren't you uncomfortable?"

"Oh, yes."

"I highly recommend nudity for comfort," Nikki suggested.

"I agree," Carter said and stood. "Absolutely."

Nikki propped herself on one elbow and watched Carter struggle out of his shorts and briefs.

Within moments, he stood before her, proudly male. She opened her arms and he lay between them, kissing not her mouth—or even her earlobes—but her breasts, making her nearly mad with desire.

"*Carter.*" His name was packed with more than three years of longing and frustration and one evening of erotic poker. She wrapped her legs around him. "*Now.*"

Holding her gaze with his, Carter positioned himself.

Nikki saw everything she'd ever wanted to see in his eyes—desire, surrender, mastery, passion...alarm. Alarm?

"What is it?" She was going to make medical history by actually expiring from sexual frustration.

"I...you haven't been...you aren't..."

Carter was obviously a man on the edge. Nikki tightened her legs.

"Nikki, I'm not wearing anything."

"I *know.*" She raked his buttocks with her nails.

"And you are?" he persisted, making her more intensely annoyed than she'd ever been in her life.

"Of course not," she snapped. What was wrong with him?

"First-aid kit still in the galley?" Sweat beaded on his forehead and his arms shook.

"Yes...are you all right?" He looked as though he was in agony. As though he were having a heart attack.

She'd teased him too much. His heart couldn't stand the strain. "Carter? Is it your heart?"

"Definitely," he gasped, then heaved himself off the bunk and ran out.

"Carter!" Nikki scrambled after him. "There's nothing in the first-aid kit for heart attacks! We'll have to radio the Coast Guard!"

She caught up with him as he pried open the plastic first-aid case and dumped the contents all over the counter. "I packed this kit for emergencies," he said, breathing heavily, but not clutching his chest.

"What kind of emergency are you having?"

"A sexual emergency," he said, finding what he was looking for.

"Oh. Oh!" Thank goodness one of them was able to think clearly. "Then you're all right?"

"Not yet."

He chased her back to the cabin. Nikki dived onto the bunk and Carter followed seconds later.

"Where were we?" he asked.

"We were at the 'now' part, and I mean *now*," she insisted, wrapping her legs around him once more.

"Yes, ma'am." He grinned. "We aim to please."

"Then you're aiming high," Nikki gasped, guiding him to her.

"Careful Nikki . . . I can't wait . . ."

She pushed herself forward. "Neither can I . . ."

Twin gasps sounded in the cabin.

"Ni-kki . . . I've been such an idiot."

"I love it when you talk sexy. Now *move!*"

And he did.

Nikki thought of waves cresting, of climbing mountains and falling off, and every roller coaster she'd ever been on. But mostly she thought of Carter and how right it felt to be one with him again.

Of course, they were both so frantic, they weren't one very long. She ran her hands over Carter's back, matching her slowing breathing to his. She was embarrassed by her instantaneous response, but his had been equally explosive.

Carter stroked her hair. "I wanted it to last. I wanted you to be as desperate for me as I was for you," he murmured.

Nikki, exhausted and replete, yawned. "Mission accomplished."

NIKKI ROLLED OVER. "Carter? Is that you?"

"Who else? Flipper?"

"Possibly. I think I found a fin."

"What a coincidence. We have un-fin-ished business."

CARTER ROLLED OVER. "Nikki? What time is it?"

"Time for love."

"I, ah, don't think I can . . . what are you doing?"

"Interesting terrain down here."

"Nikki, ah, Nikki, dear . . . that tickles."

"Mmm. How's this?"

"Darling one, I appreciate your . . . efforts, hmm, your enthusiasm . . . however, I really think . . . think . . ."

"Mmm."

"This . . . might be a case of the spirit being will-ing . . . *Nikki!*"

"There's nothing weak about *that* flesh."

"IT'S MORNING." But what time in the morning, Nikki wondered, alarmed by the bright sunlight.

"I know." Carter didn't sound worried.

She lay on her back. Carter lay beside her, also on his back. Neither moved.

"Are you hungry?"

"Ravenous," Carter said. "For food."

"Yes, food."

"One can't live on love alone."

"We certainly tried." Nikki chuckled, then groaned. "I ache in every muscle I possess."

"Believe me, the muscles you possessed ache, too."

In unison, they both laughed, then moaned.

"Carter?"

"Shh. Go back to sleep."

"But it's Monday morning. Maybe Monday mid-morning." Nikki squinted at the sunlight. "Perhaps even Monday noon."

"So?"

She was going to hate herself. "Stocks. Belden In-dustries. Takeovers. Julian. Saunders. Bob."

"I like that Bob. He's got spunk."

"If we don't contact them, they'll come out here and find us like this."

"Where's the sheet?"

"Carter!" Nikki sat up and tugged at his arm.

"Okay, okay." He winced, then sat up on the other side of the bunk. "Where's my watch?"

"It's probably on the dinette table," Nikki said, risking a glance at the captain's clock on the bulkhead behind them. "Oh, my God, it's ten-fifteen!"

The stock markets had been trading for hours. Julian and Saunders would be frantic. Nikki held her breath, even now imagining she heard the grating roar of an outboard motor.

Carter would hate her. He'd lose Belden Industries to the Karrenbrock clan. Why, oh why, didn't she keep her clothes on last night?

"Ten-fifteen?"

She looked at him warily.

"Past time for coffee, then." He stretched and stood. "I'll make it." Walking to the doorway, he paused and looked back at her.

Her apprehension must have shown in her face, for he gave her a lazy smile and said, "By the way, I wouldn't have traded last night for anything."

"But—"

"No matter what," he said firmly and headed for the galley.

A warm glow started deep inside her and spread through her body, easing her sore muscles. Carter had never said anything like that to her before. Ever. Nikki hadn't realized it was possible for her to fall deeper in love with him, but she did and knew she'd cherish his words forever.

"CALM DOWN, Saunders." Carter winced and reduced the volume on the radio.

Behind him, he heard Nikki at the door of the pilot-house. "Should we sail in?" She handed him a plate of eggs garnished with several rolling cherry tomatoes.

"Sounds like it," he answered, cutting through Saunders's diatribe. "This looks great." Carter couldn't remember the last time he was this hungry. He took a mouthful, then reached an arm around Nikki's waist and pulled her next to him.

"Are things really bad?" she asked.

Carter swallowed and sipped his coffee. "They can't buy any stock. Karrenbrock has abandoned secrecy and has made an open offer for shares. Julian is fielding calls from reporters."

"I'm sorry, Carter."

"Don't be." He smiled to show her he was sincere.

The surprising thing was that he *was* sincere. He'd imagined himself in the position of fighting off takeover bids in the past and had always felt queasy.

He supposed the queasiness would come later.

"What are you going to do?"

He grinned up at her. "I'm going to eat my eggs, drink my coffee, stare out at the ocean and think."

She pulled a storage locker out and sat on it. "May I think with you?"

"Sure. I can use thinkers right now. Saunders isn't thinking, he's ranting and raving." Carter speared a cherry tomato. "I don't suppose he'd let me talk to Julian."

Nikki turned up the volume.

"...expect us to do?"

"Saunders," Nikki answered him, "let us talk with Julian."

"He's still sending up a smoke screen."

"What about Bob?" Carter suggested. "I wonder if he's a thinker?"

"Bob is a reacter," Nikki told him. "He doesn't do well under stress."

"Too bad." Carter took the microphone from her. "Saunders, add up all the outstanding shares for me, okay? Let me know the magic number."

"I'll get right on it, Carter." The relief in Saunders's voice sounded clearly through the tinny speakers.

Chuckling, Carter ate the rest of his eggs.

"You know how many shares you need already, don't you?" Nikki guessed.

"Within a few hundred, yes. But that'll give him something to do."

"Unfortunately, it might come down to a few hundred shares." She took his plate. "I'll wash up and we can hoist anchor."

Carter held up his hand. "Wait a bit. What is your take on all this? We now know for sure that Karrenbrock wants my company. But he started acquisition *before* I was to marry his daughter, a daughter of whom he appears to be very fond. Why would he do that? It would cause horrible friction."

Nikki shrugged. "You always said you thought it was a wedding gift. Now, of course, he's angry and is out for blood."

Tapping his coffee mug, Carter gazed at the horizon. "I've changed my mind about the wedding gift. All I need is one share over fifty percent for control. If Karrenbrock wanted to ensure that I had control, he already had it within his means. He didn't have to buy more stock."

"Maybe he just wanted to have a say in how Belden is run. After all, you were going to be part of the family." Nikki stared at her coffee, her forehead wrinkling. "Maybe he was thinking of the future—his grandchildren."

"Mmm. There's a difference between a seat on the board and being chairman. He was then and he is now out for control." Carter stared at the rhythmic swelling of the waves. "But why?" he asked, thinking aloud. "He runs a conglomerate. He wouldn't have time to involve himself in the daily business of my group."

"Dee Ann would."

Propping the yellow mug next to the radio, Carter turned away from the horizon to face her. "I know you didn't think much of her goals in life, but Dee Ann was interested in securing a certain type of life-style." He shrugged. "So was I."

Nikki opened her mouth, then stopped, her eyes widening. At the same moment, a thought occurred to Carter.

"Future Security!" they said simultaneously.

"By George, I think we've got it." Carter grabbed the microphone.

"Are you thinking Future Security is a company?" she asked, pulling the locker closer to the radio.

Nodding, Carter glanced back at her, seeing the excitement in her eyes, and knowing it was reflected in his own, as well. It was beginning, this bubbling of collaboration that had always defined their relationship—

until recently. "Julian? Saunders? Anybody around? Bob?"

"Carter, old man," came back Julian, "it's not nice to abandon your executives to the wolves."

"Been bad, has it, Julian?"

"Costly."

Carter winced.

"I increased our buyback offer by five dollars a share."

"Five dollars!" Carter yelled, pegging the meter on the radio.

"We've got to pry some of those shares loose. Karrenbrock is snapping them all up."

Carter rubbed his temple.

Nikki poked him. "Future Security."

"Thanks." He squeezed her knee. "Julian, look for a company called Future Security. Find out who's on their charter. Have Bob see if they're doing any trading."

"A *company.* Of course. Fax Austin. No, I don't know where Bob is," they heard him say to someone in the background. "My apologies, Carter. You haven't lost your touch."

During the silence, Carter turned to Nikki, surprising them both by kissing her hard.

SHE DIDN'T KNOW what that was for, but she'd take it, Nikki thought, storing up memories. Carter loved challenges. This was where it all began—Carter feeling exhilarated and kissing her.

Unfortunately, the explosion of feeling couldn't last, she was sure, and she suspected that Carter wasn't willing to build anything more substantial to sustain their relationship.

Nikki shifted, forgetting about the dishes on her lap. They clattered to the deck.

Carter broke the kiss and retrieved them. "After this is all over," he said, handing them to her, "we've got to talk."

She found herself nodding, then carried the plates back to the galley. *After* this is all over, he'd said.

She should be thrilled, but a voice inside her pointed out that she'd always been *after* Belden Industries and probably always would be.

Scraping the dishes in the galley, Nikki smiled to herself. Except for last night, when for once, she'd been *before* Belden Industries.

Carter spent the next few hours in the pilothouse as Nikki prepared to get under way. As long as the reporters hadn't discovered their beach-house location, Julian thought it would be all right for Carter and Nikki to sail in. Although it had been accidental, setting up a command station away from Belden Industries offices had proved to be the best decision they'd made in a while.

Nikki carried the last of the lemonade up to Carter in time to hear Saunders's latest transmission.

"Charter papers were filed for Future Security last week. Assets are in stock."

"Gee, I wonder whose," Nikki muttered.

"Shh."

Hunched over a notepad, Carter scribbled furiously. Nikki quietly resumed her seat on the locker.

"Give me that," they heard, then Julian spoke, "Guess who is president, no other officers listed?"

"Victor Karrenbrock," Carter said.

"Wrong."

Carter sat up straight. "Who?" he asked, then, with an annoyed exclamation, depressed the microphone button. *"Who?"*

"Dee Ann Karrenbrock."

Carter's expression was priceless and one Nikki had never seen on his face before. He was stunned. Completely surprised. Clearly, he'd never considered it possible that his fiancée was anything other than what she'd presented herself to be.

Carter Belden did not have a stellar record in judging women, Nikki noted, feeling a disloyal sense of satisfaction. He'd never thought to look beneath the surface.

He hadn't with her, either.

And he hadn't with Julian. Feeling a little stunned, herself, Nikki had a revelation. Carter never looked for deception in personal relationships because he offered no deception, himself.

Business was something else entirely. There, he expected ulterior motives and delighted in uncovering them. But people? Carter was too trusting. Who'd have thought it?

Nikki tuned back into the conversation.

"She's buying blocks of shares," Julian was informing them. "Future Security has already matched our five-dollar increase."

"Increase it five more."

"Uh, Carter," Nikki said. "As your financial officer, I have to advise you—"

"I'll get the money."

Yeah, where? Nikki wondered. She held out her hand for the microphone. "I want to talk with Bob."

Carter surrendered the microphone.

"Julian, let me talk with Bob," Nikki said. Carter was going to need cash and it was her job to find it for him.

"We don't know where he is."

She and Carter exchanged looks. "You two are there by yourselves?"

"You got it."

Only now did Nikki hear the weariness in Julian's voice. "Carter, I can't stay here and do nothing. They need me."

He was already nodding. "I'll help with the anchor in just a second."

BY THE TIME they docked the *Honey Bee*, Victor Karrenbrock had transferred the majority of his holdings in Belden Industries to Future Security.

Nikki was surprised when Carter stayed until the *Honey Bee* was secure. She would have expected him to abandon ship and race to Command Central. It was true that he didn't speak much, but the fact that he stayed to help her filled Nikki with encouragement.

Things were different now, weren't they?

The beach house was a short walk away, which was good, since both Nikki and Carter were loaded down with files, papers and assorted computer equipment they'd brought from the boat. The sun was beaming down as they left the dock and stepped onto the hard-packed sand road.

The small A-frame house was built on stilts, as were most of the oceanfront houses. Carter entered without knocking.

Julian was talking on the phone, his feet propped up, his eyes closed. He was wearing the same clothes he'd worn to the *Honey Bee* on Sunday and he needed a shave.

Julian unshaven. It was unthinkable. In fact, at one time, Nikki had wondered if hair even grew on his face.

Saunders, his finger stuck in his ear, talked on another telephone. He needed a shave, too. But while the dark stubble added an attractively dangerous edge to Julian's suave good looks, Saunders just looked unkempt.

"Relax," Carter announced. "The cavalry has arrived."

Neither man paid any attention to him.

Nikki mimed a telephone at Saunders and he pointed. A cellular. *She* had a cellular. What she wanted was a secure line to go money hunting for Carter.

Julian hung up first. "Congratulations. You own the hottest stock on Wall Street."

"How much of it do I own?"

"Eight hundred shares more than you did this morning."

"That's all?" Carter paced like a caged animal. He glanced at Nikki. "Bump up the offer another three bucks."

"*Carter!*" Nikki dug for her cellular. She had to talk to Bob, secure line or not.

"Too late." Julian covered his face with his hands and massaged his eyes. "I already increased it five."

"Julian!"

"Nikki, there aren't that many shares left to buy."

Carter sat on a sofa so fast, Nikki wondered if his legs had collapsed. "Doesn't matter," he said. "I'll sell my condo if I have to."

Carter's face was ashen. Nikki addressed her next suggestion to Julian. "Can we find a white knight?"

"There was no one with enough cash to threaten Karrenbrock for us. My one nibble backed off. Not enough time to put together a deal." If anything, the bleakness in Julian's eyes was more frightening than the grayness in Carter's face.

"Is Bob at the office?" she asked, flipping open her phone. She passed by Saunders and grabbed one of his legal pads, then seated herself at the opposite end of the kitchen table.

"Bob has abandoned us."

"That's odd," Carter commented from the sofa. Nikki hadn't been certain he'd been listening. "If I were in his position, I'd be spending every second right here insinuating myself into this circle."

"Maybe he's sick," Nikki suggested.

"Too sick to call?" Carter shook his head. "I don't like it."

"Carter," Julian drawled, dropping his feet to the floor, "you have bigger problems."

"*Damn!*"

Everyone looked at Saunders as he slammed down the telephone. "I just had eighteen hundred shares, *eighteen hundred,* snatched out from under me," he lamented. "The only other large chunk of stock belongs to a Robert Smith. Do you have any idea how many Robert Smiths there are in the Galveston-Houston area?"

Nobody answered. Saunders moaned.

"How bad is it?" Carter asked quietly.

"Let's put it this way—the Karrenbrocks now own more of your company than you do. However, your stocks, added to those of everybody in this room, plus the employees, will still give you control. But you don't have fifty percent."

"How much do the employees own?"

"Less than one percent," Nikki answered. That was her bailiwick.

Carter got to his feet. "Saunders, keep trying to buy stock. Find Robert Smith. Offer him anything. Julian, you and I will personally call every employee who owns shares in Belden Industries and secure their vote or buy back their stock. Nikki, find me money."

After several hours, a punchy Saunders collapsed in the back bedroom. Julian fell asleep on the sofa with the phone in his hand.

Nikki and Carter worked long into the night, with Carter contacting as many of his employees as he could. Half the time, he'd found that they'd already sold their stock. The money offered by Future Security was too good to pass up.

"Since when does loyalty have a price?" Carter demanded, quite obviously taking the stock sales as a personal betrayal.

Nikki's neck hurt. "They're not thinking loyalty. They just see an opportunity to make a profit. Hasn't everyone you've called been surprised to hear from you?"

He nodded, resigned.

She stood, walked over to him and rubbed his neck and shoulders. "Come on. We've done all we can until tomorrow morning. Let's go back to the *Honey Bee* and go to bed."

He stretched and smiled for the first time in hours. "To sleep or to bed?"

Nikki leaned down and nibbled his ear. "To bed."

11

EARLY THE NEXT MORNING, Carter and Nikki, arms linked around each other's waists, walked back to the beach house. Nikki was absorbing the ocean sounds of crying gulls, waves lapping and breezes whispering through the sea grass, when a car, badly in need of a tune-up, pulled into the crushed-shell driveway.

"Company," Nikki said, not recognizing the car.

Carter put out a warning hand. "Reporters?"

"I hope not." That was all they needed now.

But as they watched, Bob emerged, shut the door, visibly pulled himself together and climbed the wooden steps.

Nikki started to call to him, but was silenced by Carter. "You'd spook him and he'd fall off the stairs."

Bob was acting very nervous, Nikki thought. He was dressed for a day at the office. Poor Bob, he never seemed to get it quite right.

Saunders opened the door for him.

By the time she and Carter arrived, an argument was in progress. Saunders was yelling and Julian had a hand in his pocket, the pose he adopted when he wanted to appear his most persuasive.

"Bob," Carter said in a jovial voice and held out his hand.

The hand Bob offered him in return looked as limp as leftover spaghetti.

"Have you had coffee this morning?" Carter glanced around.

He was attempting to diffuse the tension, Nikki knew. She'd seen him in action before.

"Thank you, no," Bob squeaked, then cleared his throat. When he spoke again, his voice was lower and more determined. "I only came to deliver this." He reached into his breast pocket and withdrew an envelope, which he presented to Carter with an unBob-like flourish.

Carter looked from it to Bob without touching the envelope. "You don't want me to take that. Let's talk."

Nikki glanced in puzzlement at Julian, whose face was particularly grim. Resignation letter, he mouthed, when he caught her look.

Bob resigning? When he'd been so concerned about his job? What about feeding his family and all that? Nikki edged closer so she could overhear the conversation.

The formerly belligerent Saunders was right beside her, now in full lawyer mode.

"There's nothing to talk about," Bob insisted, refusing to be led to a chair.

"I don't want you to make a decision you'll regret, Bob. Things are . . . intense right now, but they get that way from time to time." Carter's voice took on a crooning quality. "I've been very impressed with your work recently."

"You didn't know who I was until recently."

Unfair, Nikki thought. Bob underestimated Carter's knowledge of his staff.

But Carter didn't argue with him. "Well, I certainly know now." Carter went so far as to clap Bob on the shoulder.

He flinched.

"Why don't you keep this," Carter tapped the envelope, "and think about it until Friday."

Bob shook his head and placed the envelope on the coffee table. "I've already accepted another position."

"Verbal?" Saunders inquired, ever the lawyer.

"I don't believe that's your concern," Bob said in a surprising show of strength.

"My concern is to find out why you were unhappy at Belden Industries," Carter said. "Are other employees dissatisfied?"

"Dissatisfied? They may enjoy druggings, kidnappings, intrusive work hours and being patronized by the inner circle, but I do not." His chin quivered. "I've worked for you for fourteen years. Until this past weekend, I believed in the strong management and sound financial decisions you made. Part of every paycheck I drew, I used to buy stock."

"Stock?" three voices sounded in unison.

"How much stock?" Saunders asked.

Bob threw back his shoulders. "Five hundred and forty-three shares," he reported proudly.

Into the stunned silence, Julian murmured, "Robert Smith."

"Yes?" Bob turned to him even as Saunders raced for a telephone.

"We'll buy them from you and pay a five-dollar per share premium," Carter said.

"Ha!" was Bob's answer.

Not many people laughed in Carter's face and survived unscathed. His fingers clenched and relaxed. "Name your price."

His confidence clearly waning, Bob edged to the door. "I just sold my stock to Future Security for one hundred and twenty dollars a share."

Carter blinked and Nikki was amazed at his self-control. "I accept your resignation effective immediately. Now get out."

Aided by Julian, Bob scuttled to the door. Just before launching himself through it, he managed to deliver one more blow, "Please forward my mail to Karrenbrock Ventures. I believe you know the address."

Carter took a step forward, Nikki clinging to his arm to restrain him.

The door banged and they all heard Bob's footsteps pounding down the stairs.

"A hundred and twenty a share?" Saunders repeated. "That's ninety above our highest offer!"

Nikki ran to the laptop computer. Had she figured Robert Smith's shares in the employee figures?

Julian shut the door.

Carter stood at the window and looked down on Robert Smith, aka Bob the Traitor. The grinding of the starter motor sounded clearly, the car engine hiccuped and he took off.

"He ought to be able to replace that car now," Julian said.

Nikki punched in figures, then punched them in again, conscious that everyone was waiting for her tally.

After three times, the result was the same: at that moment, Carter Belden and friends controlled forty-nine point seven two eight three percent of his own company's stock.

But not fifty percent.

Nikki didn't know what to say. Trying to find the words, she stared at the screen. But all she saw were numbers. Raising her eyes, she looked directly at Carter and found that she didn't need words at all.

His shoulders slumped and he visibly deflated. Turning away from them all, he gazed out the window again.

"That's that then," Julian said.

From the other end of the table, Saunders said, "You know, I always thought Bob's eyes were set too close together."

THEY HELD the wake that evening after retrieving the death notice Victor Karrenbrock had delivered to Carter's office.

"This calls for a serious wine," Julian said, checking their stores.

"Yeah, while we can still afford it," Saunders grumbled. He'd raided the pantry, found a bag of marshmallows and he'd been staring at the telephone and eating marshmallows one by one ever since.

Carter had taken Nikki's computer and had walked down to the *Honey Bee*. Nikki wanted to follow him, but thought she'd give him some time alone.

In the meantime, she read Karrenbrock's message yet another time. "Whereas over fifty percent of outstanding Belden Industries stock is held or controlled by Karrenbrock Ventures and Future Security, Victor Karrenbrock of Karrenbrock Ventures and Dee Ann Karrenbrock of Future Security hereby call a meeting of the board of directors of Belden Industries for Friday, July 2, at 10:00 a.m. for the stated purpose of electing a new chairman."

The phone rang. Saunders answered it. After a moment, he said, "Sorry. At present, we are only offering seventeen and a quarter per share." He rolled his eyes and pulled a legal pad to him. "That was this morning. The price has dropped. In fact, I'll now offer you fifteen. Take it or leave it." Seconds later, he hung up the phone.

"Was that wise?" Julian inquired, reading a label on the bottle of red wine he held.

"She should have got it while the getting was good." Saunders popped another marshmallow into his mouth.

"Oh, look." Julian held up the bottle. "I personally know this complements roast beef, hearty stews and marshmallows."

"I'm going to be sick," Nikki said.

Pounding sounded on the wooden stairs. Nikki, being closest to the window, looked outside. "Saunders, did you phone out for pizza?"

"Nope."

"I'll tell him he's made a mistake." Nikki opened the door to a teenager peering out from behind a stack of square boxes. "I'm sorry, but you've got the wrong house," she said.

"No, he doesn't," said a voice behind him. Carter took the boxes and walked inside. Digging in his pocket, he paid the delivery boy.

"I don't carry change for any bill larger than a twenty," the youth said.

"I know. Keep it." Carter waved and closed the door.

"Wow!" they heard, followed by racing footsteps as if the boy thought Carter would change his mind.

Carter carried the boxes into the kitchen and set them on the counter. "Dinner is served."

Nikki wasn't hungry. Her heart nearly broke to see the positive front Carter put up. He was trying to rally them all and she supposed she should support him.

"I believe I'll just have the wine," Julian pronounced.

"Great!" Carter opened and closed cabinets looking for suitable glasses. Finding them, he grabbed four.

"Technically, those are white-wine glasses," Nikki heard Julian say as she slipped into the kitchen for plates.

"Oh, God forbid, Julian," Saunders said, his words muffled by marshmallows.

Nikki took the lawyer a plate and engaged in a small tug-of-war with the bag of marshmallows before he relinquished it.

After they had all selected slices of pizza, they joined Saunders at the table.

"I'd like to propose a toast," Carter said, raising his glass. "To the information superhighway—may we have a profitable trip."

What was he talking about?

As they all hesitated, Carter smiled and explained, "I've got a plan."

THE PLAN INVOLVED lots of work and no sleep, as did most of Carter's plans. The pizza should have tipped her off, Nikki thought as she trudged into the kitchen for water at about three o'clock in the morning.

Throughout the night, they'd been researching the entire Karrenbrock Ventures network, searching for weak links. Searching for anything they could use as leverage at Friday's board meeting.

By noon the next day, Nikki had to sleep. Saunders was snoring, but Julian and Carter, wearing twin looks of determination and stubble, kept tapping away on their computers.

On Wednesday, they'd installed two more phone lines, one of which was dedicated to a fax machine.

Nikki became the phone spokesperson. It seemed that people responded more favorably to a female voice and were more forthcoming with information.

After a five-hour chunk of sleep, they all awoke to a mass of charts, files, printouts and fax curls.

"Breakfast!" sounded outside the door, accompanied by a knock. The pizza guy was free-lancing as an errand boy.

Nikki opened the door and traded him a sack of dirty laundry for a sack of groceries. After a couple of days, she was sick of fast food.

"I'm going to fix us a healthy breakfast and lunch," she announced.

The others grunted.

Nikki looked around the kitchen at the fast-food containers and paper plates. The place was a sty. They hadn't opened the curtains for days.

Neither had they made any appreciable progress in hours.

"The answer's got to be here," Carter said, swapping one piece of paper for another.

"It's time for a break," Nikki said, clearing off the counter and bagging trash.

"We don't have time for a break," Carter said, irritated even this early in the morning.

"That's precisely when you need one most," Nikki informed him. She drew her confidence from the changes in their relationship.

"I want you three to pick up this place, open the curtains, then take out the trash on your way to the beach. Once there, you are to run, jump and frolic in the surf for a half hour, then return here for a nutritious breakfast."

"Nikki," Carter began.

"You're wasting time," she said.

Carter's lips gradually curved until she saw his first genuine smile in days. "Yes, ma'am."

By the time the trio returned, damp and sandy, she had breakfast ready. They grumbled at the fruit and fat-free muffins and sneered at the turkey bacon, but they laughed and talked as they ate.

Nikki surreptitiously replaced the regular coffee with decaf and sent them back to work.

After cleaning up by herself—just this once, she promised—she joined them. They were sorting all the information they'd collected on each of Karrenbrock's holdings, something they probably should have done before now.

Twenty-three piles were laid out on the living-room floor. As four people sat around and stared, one pile teetered and its contents slithered to the side.

Since it was nearest Julian, he reached out to straighten it. "Hold these, Nikki," he said, separating the two stacks.

"There's not much here, is there?" she said, hefting the few papers she held.

"No, there isn't," Carter said thoughtfully. "What's the name of that company?"

"KK's Koffee Shoppe. That's coffee with a K." Nikki flipped through the papers. "It doesn't say when he acquired it."

"Where's it located?" Julian asked.

"Rocky Falls, Texas." Nikki shook her head. "He's paid taxes on it, but it's been losing money since 1973."

They all stared at each other.

"Julian," Carter said.

Julian stood and got his car keys. "I'll be back by sundown."

"WELL, Nikki, how does it feel to be the proud owner of your very own laundromat, drugstore and coffee shop?" Saunders asked as they sat on the deck of the *Honey Bee.*

"Not to mention a lovely old home on the edge of town." Carter said with a grin, his arm draped around Nikki.

"Fantastic." To cover their tracks, Nikki Morrison was the buyer of record. Since she and Carter were still legally married, the property would fall under the Texas community property laws. She and Carter would be joint owners.

Saunders, in a shining example of why he was Carter's lawyer, pushed the contracts through in record time.

"But what if it doesn't work?" Nikki asked, still overwhelmed by the speed at which everything had happened.

"Since you and Carter used your personal funds, this property is not part of Belden Industries. Karrenbrock can't control it, so you'd become Rocky Falls's newest business tycoons."

Nikki very much hoped the plan worked.

"And now a toast," Julian said. "To sentiment."

"To sentiment," the others echoed.

This time, they drank champagne.

NIKKI AND THE OTHERS were full of confidence as they breezed into the board of directors meeting called by Victor Karrenbrock. They were gambling, but Carter was convinced they held the winning hand.

Nikki couldn't remember being happier. She'd only *thought* she was happy when Carter first noticed her years ago, but now she knew what true happiness was.

Last night, after their toast, Carter had matter-of-factly informed the others that he and Nikki would be sleeping on the *Honey Bee*. Of course, that was only partly true, but neither she nor Carter, as he told her, felt the slightest bit tired this morning.

Smiling to herself, Nikki took a seat at the conference table next to where Carter would sit. She was entitled, both as an officer of the company and as a major shareholder.

Carter had abandoned his usual grand-entrance power display in favor of personally greeting those who were present and seeing that everyone had coffee or water.

As she watched him work the room, Nikki admired the way he won over the newcomers. They were Karrenbrock's people and would vote against Carter, but now they'd feel guilty doing so.

The Karrenbrocks were late. Very late. So late, they'd crossed the line from making a look-how-important-I-am statement to a your-time-isn't-worth-as-much-as-mine statement. Not an auspicious beginning.

Carter slipped quietly into his chair at the head of the table, as if to point out that *he* was ready for business. Julian and Saunders, responding to the unspoken signal, also took their seats. Nikki was already seated because she wanted it clear that she was a participant and not a clerk or secretary.

She swiveled the plush chair and caught Carter's eye. Touching her throat, she smiled just for him.

The answering gleam in his eyes told her he understood.

After Julian and Saunders had left the *Honey Bee*, Carter had given her another gold chain. Nikki had been thrilled that he'd managed the surprise while he'd been so caught up in the takeover.

Waiting was boring. Glancing around at the other board members, Nikki slipped her shoe off and extended her leg, running her toes along Carter's calf.

And that was when the door opened and a tall blonde entered, followed by a gray-haired man with black eyebrows.

Nikki took one look at Dee Ann Karrenbrock's suit and panicked.

Faultlessly attired in a navy blue designer suit cut to perfection, Dee Ann radiated self-confidence and poise. Not by the slightest hesitation, stare or flush, did she betray her feelings upon seeing Carter for the first time since their wedding.

Come to think of it, she hadn't seen him at the wedding, had she?

But Nikki had and, though she tried to prevent it, felt a flush spread over her chest and throat.

Dee Ann and her father greeted everyone, working the room much as Carter had, and took their places at the foot of the table. Dee Ann wielded her briefcase like a pro. Another warning.

Nikki glanced at Julian, who had on his board-meeting face. Saunders was fiddling, lining up his pencils just so.

Carter looked serious, but not concerned. *Be concerned*, Nikki telegraphed mentally. *Look at her suit!*

Men could be so dense sometimes.

Dee Ann's suit was a working woman's suit, not a ladies-who-lunch suit. Although it was obviously expensive, it wasn't new. It had been worn. And the edges of her leather briefcase also showed wear. There was nothing shabby about it, but it, too, had been used.

Dee Ann's whole attitude bespoke a woman who knew her way around a boardroom.

This was the woman Carter thought wouldn't have any interest in his company? Had it ever occurred to him to wonder why she wanted ten percent of his stock?

"Thank you all for coming today," Victor began. "Carter, I'm glad to see you could make it. We weren't certain your health would permit it."

"Oh, I've fully recovered. Something I ate or drank didn't agree with me. Pretty much knocked me out," he added.

Quit making jokes and pay attention, Nikki thought.

"Let's get right to business," Victor said, reaching for the papers Dee Ann handed him. Glancing at them, he nodded and gave them to the secretary. He waited until they were distributed before continuing. "Before you are figures supporting my claim to controlling interest in Belden Industries. My personal holdings count for some twenty percent. The other nearly thirty-one percent is held by Future Security, a corporation headed by my daughter, Dee Ann. We call for the election of a new chairman of the board."

Victor sat back and laced his hands together.

Nikki scanned the figures, but found nothing she didn't already know. "Carter Belden holds just over thirty-eight percent, making him still the majority shareholder," Nikki stated. "An election is unnecessary." As if the Karrenbrocks would listen to her.

"I'm prepared to transfer the shares necessary to make my daughter majority shareholder." Raising his voice, Victor intoned, "I hereby nominate Dee Ann Karrenbrock as chairman of Belden Industries."

"Second," said one of the Karrenbrock minions.

Saunders cleared his throat. "I move the motion be tabled until after the stock transfer."

"Let's vote." Victor and his daughter wore twin smiles.

The vote went as expected, although Nikki would have thought Dee Ann would want to nail down that stock transfer from her father.

"Before we vote on the chairmanship, or should I say chairwomanship," Julian drawled, "may I know the pretty lady's qualifications? After all, Carter Belden built this company and has run it superbly."

Julian's voice dripped with patronization. Though she knew he was being a jerk on purpose, Nikki was incensed on behalf of all women. It was unfortunate that Dee Ann would have to be included in that group, but if Julian made any more cracks like that, Nikki might vote for Dee Ann, herself.

Dee Ann seemed unperturbed. "Of course. I have an MBA from the University of Texas."

A master's in business administration? Nikki stared.

Dee Ann rattled off a list of growing responsibilities within her father's company spanning eight years. As Victor Karrenbrock looked on indulgently, Dee Ann listed her achievements.

It was an eye-opening recitation and Julian's eyes were open. So were Saunders's and Carter's.

"Three years ago, I retired from the business world in order to devote time to other pursuits."

"Dee Ann," Carter said into the silence, "why didn't you tell me any of this?"

"Why didn't you ask?" Her gaze was clear—and deadly.

"Now, children," Victor chastised them, "we have a motion on the floor."

"I don't believe there is anyone here who is in doubt of the vote's outcome," Carter said, leaning forward and idly picking up a gold pen. "However, I want to assure everyone that while I will see to a smooth transition, I am not interested in running Belden Industries for someone else."

"Always assuming that I'd keep you on, Carter," Dee Ann purred. "Or any of you," she added, sweeping her gaze around their end of the table. "I, of course, have my own legal counsel," she nodded toward Saunders, "and a new hire, Robert Smith, will be taking over the comptroller's duties," she said, smiling faintly at Nikki.

Bob the Traitor. Nikki gritted her teeth, glad to be over her temporary feelings of affinity to Dee Ann.

"Julian—" Dee Ann's steely gaze softened "—you're welcome to stay."

Now, *that* was interesting, Nikki thought as Julian shook his head. With a glance toward Carter, he said, "We've already formed a partnership with Carter."

His gaze swiveled to Nikki.

Her cue. "I recently acquired some property in Rocky Falls, thinking to develop it. This will just move the timetable up."

"A little far from your stomping grounds, isn't it, Carter?" Victor sounded smug.

"I'm ready for new challenges," Carter announced as Victor's smirk widened. "I think the future is in revitalizing the downtown business districts of small municipalities."

After Carter spoke, Nikki turned to the Karrenbrocks, noting that everyone along the sides of the oval conference table was doing the same. They all looked like spectators at a tennis match.

Victor and his daughter exchanged glances. "Where is this property?"

"It's along Main Street, right Nikki?"

She nodded and withdrew the appropriate papers. "I'm really only interested in the location, but there are some buildings sitting on the property."

"We'll be razing them, naturally," Carter said.

"What buildings?" The smirk was gone.

Nikki consulted the paper, as though the names of the businesses were so unimportant that she'd forgotten them. "Let's see, Main Street Drugs, Louise's Laundry and KK's Koffee Shoppe."

"Damn you, Belden!" Victor pounded the table.

"They own Grandma's shop?" Dee Ann turned to her father in the first loss of composure Nikki had seen. "How? When?"

As the Karrenbrocks held a whispered conference, the man seated next to Julian spoke. "I'm ready to vote. My wife and I are going out of town—"

"It'll have to wait," Karrenbrock snapped at him. His eyes narrowed, he spoke carefully. "I see that your condo is listed as a corporate asset. Dee Ann has been looking for a place of her own. Be out by five o'clock this evening."

"No problem, except it's short notice for the post office." Carter frowned. "And I'll have to tell the current occupant of my new home that I'll be moving sooner than I'd planned."

"I'll forward your mail," Dee Ann offered.

"Great!" Carter grinned. "Let me give you my new address—8 Magnolia Road, Rocky Falls, Texas. I'll have to look up the zip code...or do you already know it?"

Father and daughter suddenly looked like that fish Nikki and Carter had chased on the *Honey Bee*—all staring eyes and working mouths.

"You're lying," Victor managed to say.

"Check it out."

A stone-faced Victor took him up on his suggestion. "I'd like to break for fifteen minutes."

"Sure." Carter spread his hands.

Babble began instantly. Julian stood and announced, "I'm going to arrange for lunch to be served in the east conference room. Please stay as our guests." He opened the door to the conference room and beckoned to someone outside. "For now, I can offer you fresh coffee and KK's special coffee cake."

With a snarl, Victor Karrenbrock stormed out of the room. Dee Ann's exit was much more dignified. Looking thoughtful, she gathered her papers, wrapped a piece of coffee cake in a napkin and followed her father.

Nikki exhaled.

Saunders groaned and rested his head on the table. "I'm too old for this stress."

"I guess so," Nikki said. "Your bald spot looks bigger than it did last week."

Immediately, his hand went to his head as he took inventory of his hair. Flushing when he saw their grins, he rose from the table. "I'm going to check and see if I have any messages."

Under cover of the noise around the coffee bar, Nikki spoke to Carter. "What do you think?"

Carter shrugged. "He's probably calling his mother right now."

"You wouldn't really turn her out of her house, would you?"

"Number one, it's our house, and number two, she got an extraordinary price for it." He gave Nikki a wry smile. "She's got a son she can go live with."

Nikki sighed and stretched out the kinks in her shoulders. "I'm counting on the fact that this will work and I won't have beggared myself for nothing." If it didn't work, she'd have to borrow to pay the docking fees for the *Honey Bee* and her rent. Heck, she'd end up living on the *Honey Bee*.

"It'll work." Carter reached across the table and squeezed her clenched fists. "Relax."

"I think I'm going to eat coffee cake."

"Bring me a piece, will you?"

It wasn't long before a furious Victor Karrenbrock returned to the conference room. "I'd like to speak with you privately," he informed Carter.

Julian led everyone to the east conference room for lunch. Saunders returned to the room, beaming, as did Dee Ann.

"Saunders." Carter beckoned to him. "Victor, I'm assuming that by 'private' you weren't excluding my counsel or Ms. Morrison, who owns the property in question."

Nikki tried to look like a property owner to be reckoned with.

"You're Carter's first wife, aren't you?" Dee Ann asked.

"Yes."

"Congratulations. Do tell me how you managed to get him to the altar."

"Well, actually I didn't. I got him to a beach and we were married there."

"Ah." Dee Ann nodded. "Is that what I did wrong?"

"Dee Ann, don't demean yourself." Victor cleared his throat. "It appears that I underestimated you, Carter. You're even more devious than I am."

"I think not," Carter drawled.

"You are depriving an elderly woman of her livelihood. For over fifty years, Katrina Karrenbrock has run KK's. It's a Rocky Falls landmark."

"But it isn't a profitable landmark."

"That's not the point!" Victor reined in his temper. "It's a place where she can gab with her friends. She feels useful. Don't take that away from her."

Carter appeared to be giving his words serious consideration. "Are you making an offer for the property?"

"Name your price."

"I think you know my price."

"No." The hard voice was Dee Ann's. "Grandma is getting older. In a few years, she won't be able to run the coffee shop. This is for the best."

Victor turned to her. "It's not just Mama. Didn't you hear? He's got Louise's place and the drugstore. Tony's boy is the new pharmacist. It'll all be gone."

"Dad, Grandma *sold* it to them."

"They tricked her."

Dee Ann shoved a paper under his nose. "For those prices? She'd have been a fool *not* to sell."

"Don't talk about your grandmother that way!"

"Dad." Dee Ann leaned forward earnestly. "Think about this—about what we've worked toward."

Victor shook his head. "You aren't going to marry the guy now, so we'll find another company." Nodding to Carter, he said again, "Your price?"

"I'll swap the Rocky Falls properties for an equivalent amount in Belden stock—current value, of course."

Which was considerably less than during the crazy trading earlier in the week.

"I took the liberty," Saunders said, pushing a paper toward Victor.

He, in turned, pushed it toward Dee Ann.

She shook her head. "I'm not interested in buying property in Rocky Falls."

Dee Ann was going to bear watching, Nikki thought. This was the woman who was prepared to marry for reasons other than love and who appeared to lack any sentiment whatsoever. She was also smart and had extensive business experience.

And she had a huge grudge against them all.

After her statement, Dee Ann stared at her father. He stared back. And he turned away first.

"Let's talk numbers, gentlemen."

Nikki decided to overlook the slight.

Unfortunately, the numbers weren't kind to Victor Karrenbrock. The stock's value had plunged to levels approaching those prior to the takeover attempt. His twenty percent holdings weren't enough. Dee Ann would have to relinquish some of her stock, as well.

Victor turned to his daughter. "Dee Ann, baby, it's your grandmother."

"And she's got enough money now so that she never has to work again. Her future is set."

"But what kind of a future will it be with her leaving her friends and her home?"

"One she *chose*."

Their eyes locked again.

"Dee Ann," her father whispered.

"You're asking me to pay for her mistake?"

"I'll make it up to you," Victor pleaded.

Dee Ann shook her head, "I don't think that's possible."

12

"YOU'VE FORGOTTEN—Carter humiliated me. He *jilted* me in front of all our friends and business associates. In front of our family."

"You were trying to take over my company!" Carter protested.

"Which," Dee Ann said, glaring at him, "we wouldn't have been able to do if you'd managed it better!"

Dee Ann had just struck a severe blow. Nikki knew that Carter blamed himself for everything, especially for jeopardizing his control. "I believe," he said carefully and quietly, "that in this affair, I have conducted myself with more consideration for your feelings than you have for mine."

"You obviously haven't been the recipient of pitying notes and visits of condolence during the past week. And I *know* you haven't had to listen to my mother's moaning."

"Dee Ann, sweetheart." Victor touched her arm. Dee Ann shook it off.

"It's unfortunate when a groom falls ill, but hardly a scandal," Carter said.

"You weren't ill."

"Actually, he was," Nikki inserted.

Dee Ann turned her icy glare toward Nikki. "I *know* it wasn't appendicitis."

Nikki ignored the images of precisely how Dee Ann would know that. "He was agitated and we overmedicated him."

"Dee Ann, I apologized," Carter said in a voice equal parts sympathy and irritation. "And I apologize again. But no more."

"Dee Ann, honey," Victor said in a conciliatory tone, "the man's not worth it. Would you have wanted to be married to a con artist?"

Her eyes were suspiciously bright. "He didn't swindle Grandma. He offered her twice what that property is worth and you know it."

"She didn't know he was going to tear it down."

"Then she shouldn't have sold it."

Victor Karrenbrock's weakness might be sentimentality, but he obviously hadn't passed those feelings along to his daughter. The man who had been Belden Industries' nemesis on occasions too numerous to remember, deflated before their eyes. "I'll give you anything you want."

"*Anything?*" Dee Ann asked sharply.

"That's what I said," Victor confirmed in a barely audible voice.

To Nikki's surprise, Dee Ann inclined her head. "Sold. How many shares do you need?"

That's going to cost him, Nikki thought as she calculated the number of shares Dee Ann would have to contribute.

Sometime during the negotiations, Julian poked his head in. "What's the status?"

Dee Ann responded. "I'm sure it will come as no surprise to you that I'm withdrawing my name from contention."

"Then I'll inform everyone the meeting is over." When no one objected, he withdrew. Nikki heard whistling.

Within a few minutes, Saunders had prepared the necessary papers.

"Just a moment," Dee Ann said, scanning them critically. "It lists the buyer as Carter Belden. The owner of record is Nikki Morrison."

"I was just trying to avoid some extra legal steps," Saunders said with a nervous laugh. "It's okay, really."

"She was just a front, then?"

Saunders nodded. "And she'll turn right around and sell the shares to Carter."

"How accommodating of her," Dee Ann said.

Everyone looked at Nikki, who found she didn't like being taken for granted or appearing the pawn in front of the surprising Dee Ann.

"Nevertheless." Tapping neutrally polished nails, Dee Ann studied her. "You own how much Belden Industries stock?"

"Six percent," Nikki told her, knowing that Dee Ann had access to the information, anyway.

"You should have negotiated for more."

"I did. I traded some for a boat."

Dee Ann raised her eyebrows. "It must be some boat."

"It is," Nikki said, smiling at Carter.

Dee Ann shrugged. "Six percent, plus twenty from my father, plus . . ." She punched numbers into a calculator. "My *twelve*," she said, glaring at her silent father, "and you'll have thirty-eight percent of Belden Industries stock. What a marvelous return on your investment."

Dee Ann and Nikki exchanged brittle smiles. "That's a substantial chunk of stock, isn't it, Carter?"

"Yes." His voice was clipped.

There was a message there, but Nikki didn't understand what it was until Dee Ann spoke again. "Goodness. *You* own about thirty-eight percent, don't you, Carter?"

"About."

Next to him, Saunders fidgeted, which was unusual when he was in his lawyer mode.

Dee Ann smiled. "Nikki, I'm throwing in an extra few shares for your trouble."

"That's not necessary," Saunders protested.

"What, are you crazy?" Victor's profit instincts were already bruised.

"No," Dee Ann said, filling in numbers and signing her name with a flourish.

She passed the paper to Nikki, who hurriedly signed it, relief making her hands sweat.

"This is *almost* as good as being chairman myself," Dee Ann said, packing up her briefcase. "Carter, your ex-wife now controls your company. Nikki, I hope you'll make the most of your opportunity."

"Oh, I will," Nikki said. There was no need to tell Dee Ann that Nikki and Carter were still married. Maybe now, the woman would go away and leave them alone.

Everyone stood and Carter spoke, "Dee Ann, why was gaining control of my company so important to you?"

Dee Ann turned to him. "I wanted children and I wanted the time to nurture them. When a woman has young children, she's vulnerable. Dependent. I've seen my friends' marriages break up and how they struggle to raise their children on their own. If my father and I controlled your company, you would never leave me. And eventually, our children would inherit the stock."

It was so logical, Nikki thought. Cold-blooded, but logical. She shivered, not because she disapproved, but because she understood so well.

Carter nodded, but Nikki wondered if *he* truly understood. "I hope you find happiness," he said, offering his hand.

Dee Ann shook it. "I intend to."

As soon as the conference-room door closed behind the Karrenbrocks, Carter gave a loud whoop and twirled Nikki in his arms.

"We did it!"

They laughed and rehashed the winning moments for several minutes before noticing that Saunders sat quietly at the table.

"Well done, Saunders!" Carter approached him, hand outstretched. "Time to celebrate."

"Well, yes." Saunders gave a weak grin, followed by an equally thin chuckle. "You can, uh, make it a double celebration." He held up a thick envelope. "Your divorce papers came yesterday."

Divorce.

Nikki clutched the back of the nearest chair. She'd forgotten. For the last few glorious days, she'd forgotten. Carter's back was to her. She wished he'd look at her, wished she knew what he was thinking.

She wished he'd snatch the envelope out of the lawyer's hand and rip up the papers into tiny pieces. Then, in the best cinematic tradition, he'd take her into his arms and throw the pieces into the air where they'd drift downward as he kissed her.

Maybe *she* could rip up the papers. Maybe Carter didn't know how she felt.

Slowly, he took the envelope and broke the seal, withdrawing blue-covered documents.

"I have one set here for you, Nikki." Saunders held up a twin of Carter's envelope.

Numbly, Nikki walked over to the table. "Do I have to sign anything?" Her voice sounded thin and reedy.

"No," Saunders said. "You already did more than three years ago."

"Oh."

Carter said nothing. Nikki wished he'd say something. Or at least look at her.

When he finally spoke, it wasn't what she'd expected. "These have Wednesday's date on them."

"They were delivered yesterday morning."

"Why wasn't I told?" Carter snapped.

"Because I just retrieved them!" Saunders snapped back. "I couldn't let the secretary open them, could I?"

"No, no, of course not." Carter ran a hand through his hair. "Let's, uh, get on with the other, then."

That was it? Wasn't Carter going to say anything about the divorce? Nikki took faint hope from his agitation. He obviously was as surprised by the papers as she was. Maybe that meant . . .

"Here you go, Nikki." Saunders handed her his favorite fountain pen.

Nikki could swear both men held their breaths as she bent over the transfer documents. What, did they think she wouldn't sign?

She glanced up and caught the watchful expression on Carter's face. She'd seen it before—always when he was about to close a deal he wanted particularly badly.

Or one in which the terms were better for him than they were for the other party and he wasn't quite certain that the other party would actually go through with the deal.

Nikki stopped and scanned the papers. She never, absolutely never, signed anything without reading it first. The only reason she'd started to now was that she thought Saunders might be insulted.

So let him be insulted.

"It's just a simple transfer, Nikki," Saunders said with a forced casualness that raised the hair on the back of her neck.

The number of shares of stock to be transferred looked huge. "Wait a minute—this transfers *all* the stock to you, Carter."

"So? That was our deal." He spoke too quickly.

What was going on? "But I owned six percent before this all started. That shouldn't be included."

Saunders exhaled. "Oops." He smiled, reached for the papers, then subtracted Nikki's six percent. He shoved the documents back to her. "That's what happens when you get in a rush." He laughed. He was the only one who did.

Something was wrong. Nikki looked from Carter to Saunders, then set down her pen and prepared to study the papers in detail. "Why did you include the entire thirty-two percent, Saunders? By virtue of the community property laws, Carter already owns half of that."

She handed the papers back to Saunders again. Instead of taking them, he shoved his hands into his pockets. Clearing his throat, he murmured. "The, ah, community property laws weren't in effect at the time of the purchase."

"Not in effect?" Nikki looked to Carter.

He stared back, unmoving, unblinking. Her gaze fell to his white-knuckled grip on the divorce papers, and with a growing disgust, she understood.

Their divorce was final before she bought the property yesterday. Dee Ann had indeed transferred controlling interest to Carter Belden's ex-wife.

And now, Carter was afraid he wouldn't get his company back. That was all their divorce meant to him. Nikki was so angry, a dark haze ringed her vision.

Nothing between them had changed at all. Those magical moments on board the *Honey Bee* might never have happened.

His company was everything to him. It always had been, and so help her, Nikki now knew it always would be.

Well, let him have his stupid company. She jerked the papers closer and blinked, trying to clear the sudden onslaught of tears. She wanted to sign before she broke down.

She got as far as N when she stopped.

If Carter had openly pointed out to her all the legal ramifications, they could have had a good laugh about it. She'd razz him a little, but they'd both know there was no possibility of Nikki actually reneging on their agreement.

But there hadn't been any jokes because he didn't trust her. He was treating her like a business adversary.

Unbidden, Dee Ann's words came back to her. *I hope you make the most of your opportunity.*

Nikki thought of the six percent Saunders had "accidentally" included. Saunders didn't make mistakes like that.

With quiet deliberation, she capped the pen. Then she took the documents, held them up and tore them in half.

"What are you doing?" Saunders shrieked as she stood.

"Nikki!" Carter tried to prevent her from leaving.

"You two are loathsome. Truly despicable."

"Nikki, be reasonable." Carter always said this when the deal was about to get away.

"I *am* being reasonable," she said, sidestepping him. "A reasonable woman wouldn't sign away her future for nothing." She thought of Dee Ann. "Just think, if I went into partnership with Dee Ann, we'd easily control over half the stock. Dee Ann had the right idea. And I've been incredibly stupid!"

"Nikki, what will it take to bring you back to the negotiating table?" Another Carterism.

"Ooh!" She snatched her purse and headed for the door.

"Champagne, anyone?" Julian entered just as Nikki was pushing past.

"Yes, thank you," she said, grabbing the bottle to take with her.

OPTIONS. She was a woman with options.

Nikki sat on the deck of her boat and drank champagne directly from the bottle. Julian would be appalled.

She didn't care. She didn't care what any of them thought of her anymore.

Nikki grabbed the railing and hoisted the bottle skyward as she threw back her head and laughed. It was of no concern *what* they thought. They, however, had better be concerned about what she thought. *She* would be calling the shots.

"Morrison Industries." That had a nice ring to it.

Naturally, Carter would quit and take the weasely Saunders with him. Bob had already quit, which left Julian.

Hmm, Julian. Nikki swigged a mouthful of champagne and tried very hard to conjure up Julian's face. It was a very nice face. Maybe she should have an affair with him. A nice, uncomplicated affair.

And when it was over, Carter would be a distant memory. As a bonus, Nikki would have a thorough knowledge of wines.

Yes, there were definite advantages to an affair with Julian.

But men stuck together, the swine. Julian would probably throw in his lot with Carter.

So...she'd call Dee Ann. Dee Ann was all right. She liked Dee Ann. Together, they'd fire all the men.

"NM Industries." To the world, it would stand for Nikki Morrison, but she and Dee Ann would know it meant "No Men."

The afternoon sun was blazing hot and the champagne was warm. Nikki set the bottle down and gazed around her boat. The *Honey Bee.* For more than three years, she'd kept the boat, always hoping for a reconciliation with Carter.

What now? Sell it? Nikki would miss her weekends. Hey, she was a wealthy woman, she could spend whole weeks on the craft if she wanted to.

She'd rechristen it. In fact, she'd rechristen it right now. Seizing the champagne bottle, she slipped her shoes back on and ran down to the dock.

Making her way to the bow, she stopped and raised the bottle. "I christen thee the *Options*," she declared and whacked the hull with the bottle.

Instead of breaking, it bounced off the Fiberglas. Champagne spurted down her arm.

As she stood, dripping, she heard footsteps behind her. "What a waste of good champagne."

Sooner or later, she'd known Carter was bound to seek her out. She'd hoped it would be later.

Nikki ignored him and splashed some champagne on the hull. "There. This boat is now officially the *Options*."

"What kind of boat name is that?"

"*My* name." Nikki began walking across the gangway, followed by Carter. "I'm going to redecorate, too. A pastel floral pattern, I think. Coral or rose. Lots of frilly feminine touches."

"Why don't you just paint the whole thing pink?"

He was awfully impertinent for someone in his position. She turned to him. "I don't recall granting you permission to come aboard."

He visibly struggled to control his irritation. "Nikki, we have to talk."

"Wrong," she said. "*I* don't have to talk to anybody." She pointed a finger at his chest. "*You're* the one who has to talk. But I don't have to listen if I don't want to."

"After all we've meant to each other—"

"Ha! Where was all this sentimental twaddle a couple of hours ago when you and Saunders were swindling me?" She flopped into a lounge chair and closed her eyes.

"We weren't swindling you. You know we only used your name to keep Karrenbrock from discovering I was connected with the Rocky Falls deal."

"Excuse me, you used my money, too."

"I would have paid you back."

"That provision was missing from the transfer document."

She heard a heavy sigh. "It should have been included."

"It wasn't, though."

"But you know I would have paid you back." His voice sounded so soothingly reasonable. Oh, she hated it when people talked like that to her.

"Just the way you knew I'd give you the stock?"

Nikki felt the sun warm her legs as Carter's shadow moved and he took the lounge chair next to her. "I've really botched things. Really screwed up."

"Yep."

"So, what do you want, Nikki?"

Tears stung her eyes. She kept them closed. "Frankly, I don't know what I want anymore. I used to know what I wanted."

"I used to know what I wanted, too," Carter said. "Are you wearing any sun block?"

"No, I'm trying for a lovely, golden tan."

"You'll burn."

"What do you care?"

"I care that thirty years from now you'll look like spotted leather."

"I doubt you'll be around to see my skin in thirty years."

There was a short silence. "But I'd like to be," he said softly.

"Oh, please." She sat up and glared at him. "Don't insult me. We both know you're terrified that I won't sign the stock over to you."

"Would you believe me if I told you I don't care about the stock?"

"No."

"I don't blame you, but it's true. This past week we've spent together has taught me—"

"Stop." She held out her hand. "I can't take any more. Just give me the papers and I'll sign them. I know you've brought a fresh set with you."

Carter took her hand and brought it to his lips. "Will you marry me?"

She snatched her hand away. "Been there, done that. Now, give me the papers, then get off my boat and get out of my life."

"No. I love you, Nikki."

The gall of the man. "There was a time when I would have given anything to hear you say that. That time has passed."

"I didn't know I was in love with you until you ran out the door of the conference room."

"Taking your stock with me."

"Yes!" He stood up and paced in front of her. "And all I thought about was that you'd been hurt by this."

"Oh, really." He was persistent, she'd give him that. Dense, but persistent.

"Yes, really!" He paused and leaned against the railing, facing her. "I was so shaken up by the divorce—I'd forgotten all about the stock."

"Me, too," Nikki admitted grudgingly.

"I know you don't want to hear this, but I wasn't really in love with you when we were married."

Nikki gasped.

"I *thought* I loved you and I did, to the extent I was capable. But the first time it looked as though there might be trouble in paradise, what happened?"

"You sent me to Mexico."

He nodded. "We rushed into marriage and we rushed out of it without giving it time to develop."

Thinking back to her own realizations, Nikki was forced to agree with him. "I never changed from Nikki-at-the-office to Nikki-the-person. We never talked about the future, never made plans, never set goals. You didn't know me at all because I was afraid to show you. You'd married my office persona and that's the one I felt I had to maintain."

"And when you tried to change, I didn't want to deal with it." Carter shook his head. "I'm sorry, Nikki. I didn't think about what marriage meant. I guess I was only trying to protect you from office gossip."

"Yeah." She hugged her knees, stung by his blunt admission.

"This last week showed me what I'd been missing. To be honest, I'm ready to work at a relationship now. I'd hoped to develop one with Dee Ann, but I made the same mistakes with her as I made with you. I didn't factor in love."

"You'll forgive me for questioning your timing." Nikki's feelings were still bruised.

"But that's exactly it!" Wind ruffling his hair, he crossed the deck to sit on the chair with her. "The first thing I thought of was you. I saw those divorce papers and I was . . . scared. I'm not afraid to admit it. I didn't know what to say to you. I didn't know what you wanted me to say and I didn't particularly want to discuss the whole thing in front of Saunders, so I tried to get the stock transfer out of the way so he'd leave." When he finished, he was out of breath.

He looked unsure of himself and Nikki liked that right now. When a man proposed, he needed to be unsure of himself. It would keep him in line, later.

Later. She wasn't seriously buying any of this, was she?

"Look." He withdrew papers, which he'd folded into squares and stuck in his shorts pocket.

Nikki smoothed them, expecting to see duplicates of the documents she'd torn earlier. She had to read the opening paragraph twice before the meaning sunk in. "It's a prenuptial agreement!"

Carter nodded. "It lets you retain your shares in Belden Industries as separate property. They'll always be yours, Nikki."

"But right now, I have controlling interest," she said.

"I know. I don't care. I want you in my life and this is the only way I can prove that I love you."

She was beginning to believe him. He was either

crazy in love with her, or just crazy. "What if we had a fight and I sold everything to Dee Ann?"

He stood. "Sell it now, then we won't have to worry about it." Smiling, he continued, "You see? Belden Industries is no longer the most important thing in my life. You are."

He leaned down and kissed her, as if reminding her what *was* most important.

Nikki sighed against his mouth. She'd needed that reminder.

"I'm going back to the office and let you think. I'm not giving up, though."

Bemused, Nikki nodded and Carter gave her one last kiss, then turned to leave.

He probably thought she'd tear up these papers, too. That was it. He was bluffing.

Well, she'd call his bluff. She'd sign the prenuptial agreement and watch his face as she did so. Then she'd know for sure what his true feelings were.

"Carter—wait!" She trotted after him. "I don't have a pen."

"You'll sign? You'll marry me?" Hope spread over his face. Patting his pockets, he murmured, "I had it clipped to the papers. Here it is." He extended it to her.

His hand trembled. Nerves? Carter?

"You sure you want to marry me?" she asked.

"I've never been more certain of anything in my life." His face was open. His hazel eyes hid no trickery.

Nikki set the papers on the life-raft canister and

scrawled her name. Just before she finished, she looked up quickly.

Carter's face was transformed by joy. He enveloped her in his arms, holding her so tightly, she had trouble breathing.

"I promise you won't regret this, Nikki."

"You really do love me," she said in wonder.

"I really love you," he echoed, accompanying his words with a kiss. "I do have one request, though."

"Anything." Nikki was feeling generous.

Carter nudged her over to the railing. "Would you consider unchristening your boat?"

"What, you don't like the *Options*?"

"No." Carter slipped his arm around her waist. "Because after we get married, we're taking the *Honey Bee* on a long honeymoon. No options."

Epilogue

THE HARPIST played softly. Waves slapped the beach. Roses and sea breezes scented the air. The golden sunset of a hot Galveston August evening filtered through the gauze of the wedding tent. Guests murmured in anticipation.

And the groom's pager beeped.

Standing at one of the tables set up for the reception, Carter Belden turned off the pager and withdrew his cellular phone.

"It's about time!" Saunders grumbled. "I've got sand in my shoes."

"Then take them off," Carter suggested as he punched out a number. "Julian?" he said into the mouthpiece.

"Nikki's on her way and so am I," Julian answered.

"Sure you won't stand beside me?" Carter asked, though Julian had steadfastly refused prior requests.

"Oh, no." Julian chuckled. "I'm staying as far away from the altar as possible."

"You'll change your mind someday and I want to be there to see it."

"Let's get you married first," Julian said before breaking the connection.

Smiling, Carter glanced at the beach house behind him where Nikki and her sister had dressed, then took his place at the back of the tent as a late-arriving guest slipped inside.

He froze. "Dee Ann!"

"Hello, Carter," she greeted him, her pumps sinking into the sand. With a stiff laugh, she held on to his arm and bent to remove her shoes.

Over her head, Carter and Saunders exchanged looks.

"That's better." Dee Ann straightened, looked first at Saunders, then at Carter and made a face. "Relax. Nikki invited me."

"I knew that," Carter said, annoyed that he hadn't.

"No, you didn't," Dee Ann contradicted cheerfully. "Nikki thought it would spike the gossips if I came to your wedding."

"Or give them something else to talk about," Saunders mumbled.

"Ah, you made it," said Julian's voice behind them.

"Am *I* the only one who didn't know Dee Ann was coming?" Carter asked in a whisper that drew the stares of the row of guests nearest him.

"*I* didn't!" Saunders said, pouting.

"Quiet," Julian commanded as he held out his arm to Dee Ann. "Nikki remembered your allergy and made sure the bouquet over here didn't have roses in it," Carter could hear him saying as he led Dee Ann toward the other side of the tent.

"Women," Carter muttered to Saunders.

But Saunders didn't reply. Carter followed his rapt gaze and saw Nikki and her sister approaching down a white runner that had been laid across the beach from the house to the tent.

He and Nikki had decided to re-create their original wedding ceremony. This time, however, Nikki's entire family was present, along with the couple's closest friends—and Dee Ann.

Nikki wore a white strapless sarong, with flowers in her hair, in her arms and looping around her neck. Her sister wore a similar sarong in dusky apricot shot with gold to imitate a beach sunset.

Carter and Julian wore white, loose-fitting tunics and pants. Only Saunders insisted on a suit and shoes. Perhaps, Carter thought, he could kick sand over them before the photographs were taken.

And then he forgot about the lawyer's shoes and everything else as Nikki walked toward him.

As the waves swelled, so did his heart. "Thank you," he whispered when she reached his side, her face luminous.

"What for?" she asked. "Not jilting you?"

He took her hand, the hand that would soon wear a gold ring. "For giving me a second chance." His lips grazed her knuckles. "This time, I'll get it right."

The minister softly cleared his throat. "Are you ready to begin the ceremony?"

In unison, two voices answered, "Yes."

* * * * *

Be sure to watch for the next installment of the
"Grooms on the Run" promotion.
NOT THIS GUY! *by Glenda Sanders*
will be available in July 1995,
wherever Harlequin books are sold.

HARLEQUIN®
Temptation®

Secret Fantasies

Do you have a secret fantasy?

America's sweetheart Josie Eastman does. She's always done what she's told, never endangered her precious career. And she's sick of it. So she drops everything and escapes into the arms of a bad-boy rancher. But soon she realizes why she was always told, "Never love a cowboy...." Enjoy #546 NEVER LOVE A COWBOY by Kate Hoffmann, available in July 1995.

Everybody has a secret fantasy. And you'll find them all in Temptation's exciting new yearlong miniseries, Secret Fantasies. Beginning January 1995, one book each month focuses on the hero and heroine's innermost romantic desires....

THREE BESTSELLING AUTHORS

HEATHER GRAHAM POZZESSERE
THERESA MICHAELS
MERLINE LOVELACE

bring you

THREE HEROES THAT DREAMS ARE MADE OF!

The Highwayman—He knew the honorable thing was to send his captive home, but how could he let the beautiful Lady Kate return to the arms of another man?

The Warrior—Raised to protect his tribe, the fierce Apache warrior had little room in his heart until the gentle Angie showed him the power and strength of love.

The Knight—His years as a mercenary had taught him many skills, but would winning the hand of a spirited young widow prove to be his greatest challenge?

Don't miss these **UNFORGETTABLE RENEGADES!**

Available in August wherever Harlequin books are sold.

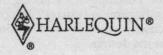

HARLEQUIN®
Temptation

THREE GROOMS:
Case, Carter and Mike

TWO WORDS:
"We Don't!"

ONE MINISERIES:

GROOMS ON THE RUN

Starting in May 1995, Harlequin Temptation
brings you an exciting miniseries called

GROOMS ON THE RUN

Each book (and there'll be one a month for three
months!) features a sexy hero who's ready to say,
"I do!" but ends up saying, "I don't!"

Watch for these special Temptations:

In May, **I WON'T!** by Gina Wilkins #539
In June, **JILT TRIP** by Heather MacAllister #543
In July, **NOT THIS GUY!** by Glenda Sanders #547

Available wherever Harlequin books are sold.

MOVE OVER, MELROSE PLACE!

> Apartment for rent
> One bedroom
> Bachelor Arms
> 555-1234

Come live and love in L.A. with the tenants of Bachelor Arms. Enjoy a year's worth of wonderful love stories and meet colorful neighbors you'll bump into again and again.

When Blythe Fielding planned her wedding and asked her two best friends, Caitlin and Lily, to be bridesmaids, none of them knew a new romance was around the corner for each of them—not even the bride! These entertaining, dramatic stories of friendship, mystery and love by JoAnn Ross continue the exploits of the residents of Bachelor Arms and answer one very important question: Will Blythe ever get to walk down the aisle? Find out in:

NEVER A BRIDE (May 1995) #537

FOR RICHER OR POORER (June 1995) #541

THREE GROOMS AND A WEDDING (July 1995) #545

Soon to move into Bachelor Arms are the heroes and heroines in books by always popular Candace Schuler and Judith Arnold. A new book every month!

Don't miss the goings-on at Bachelor Arms.

HARLEQUIN®

Don't miss these Harlequin favorites by some of our most
distinguished authors!
And now, you can receive a discount by ordering two or more titles!

HT #25607	PLAIN JANE'S MAN by Kristine Rolofson	$2.99 U.S./$3.50 CAN. ☐
HT #25616	THE BOUNTY HUNTER by Vicki Lewis Thompson	$2.99 U.S./$3.50 CAN. ☐
HP #11674	THE CRUELLEST LIE by Susan Napier	$2.99 U.S./$3.50 CAN. ☐
HP #11699	ISLAND ENCHANTMENT by Robyn Donald	$2.99 U.S./$3.50 CAN. ☐
HR #03268	THE BAD PENNY by Susan Fox	$2.99 ☐
HR #03303	BABY MAKES THREE by Emma Goldrick	$2.99 ☐
HS #70570	REUNITED by Evelyn A. Crowe	$3.50 ☐
HS #70611	ALESSANDRA & THE ARCHANGEL by Judith Arnold	$3.50 U.S./$3.99 CAN. ☐
HI #22291	CRIMSON NIGHTMARE by Patricia Rosemoor	$2.99 U.S./$3.50 CAN. ☐
HAR #16549	THE WEDDING GAMBLE by Muriel Jensen	$3.50 U.S./$3.99 CAN. ☐
HAR #16558	QUINN'S WAY by Rebecca Flanders	$3.50 U.S./$3.99 CAN. ☐
HH #28902	COUNTERFEIT LAIRD by Erin Yorke	$3.99 ☐
HH #28824	A WARRIOR'S WAY by Margaret Moore	$3.99 U.S./$4.50 CAN. ☐

(limited quantities available on certain titles)

	AMOUNT	$
DEDUCT:	**10% DISCOUNT FOR 2+ BOOKS**	$
ADD:	**POSTAGE & HANDLING**	$
	($1.00 for one book, 50¢ for each additional)	
	APPLICABLE TAXES*	$_____
	TOTAL PAYABLE	$_____
	(check or money order—please do not send cash)	

To order, complete this form and send it, along with a check or money order for the
total above, payable to Harlequin Books, to: **In the U.S.:** 3010 Walden Avenue,
P.O. Box 9047, Buffalo, NY 14269-9047; **In Canada:** P.O. Box 613, Fort Erie, Ontario,
L2A 5X3.

Name: _____

Address: _____ City: _____

State/Prov.: _____ Zip/Postal Code: _____

*New York residents remit applicable sales taxes.
Canadian residents remit applicable GST and provincial taxes.

HBACK-AJ2

ANNOUNCING THE

PRIZE SURPRISE SWEEPSTAKES!

This month's prize:

L-A-R-G-E—SCREEN PANASONIC TV!

This month, as a special surprise, we're giving away a fabulous FREE TV!

Imagine how delighted you and your family will be to own this brand-new 31" Panasonic** television! It comes with all the latest high-tech features, like a SuperFlat picture tube for a clear, crisp picture...unified remote control...closed-caption decoder...clock and sleep timer, and much more!

The facing page contains two Entry Coupons (as does every book you received this shipment). Complete and return *all* the entry coupons; **the more times you enter, the better your chances of winning the TV!**

Then keep your fingers crossed, because you'll find out by July 15, 1995 if you're the winner!

Remember: The more times you enter, the better your chances of winning!*

PTV KAL

PRIZE SURPRISE

SWEEPSTAKES

OFFICIAL ENTRY COUPON

This entry must be received by: JUNE 30, 1995
This month's winner will be notified by: JULY 15, 1995

YES, I want to win the Panasonic 31" TV! Please enter me in the drawing and let me know if I've won!

Name_____

Address_____ Apt._____

City   State/Prov.   Zip/Postal Code

Account #_____

Return entry with invoice in reply envelope.

© 1995 HARLEQUIN ENTERPRISES LTD.   CTV KAL

PRIZE SURPRISE

SWEEPSTAKES

OFFICIAL ENTRY COUPON

This entry must be received by: JUNE 30, 1995
This month's winner will be notified by: JULY 15, 1995

YES, I want to win the Panasonic 31" TV! Please enter me in the drawing and let me know if I've won!

Name_____

Address_____ Apt._____

City   State/Prov.   Zip/Postal Code

Account #_____

Return entry with invoice in reply envelope.

© 1995 HARLEQUIN ENTERPRISES LTD.   CTV KAL

OFFICIAL RULES

PRIZE SURPRISE SWEEPSTAKES 3448

NO PURCHASE OR OBLIGATION NECESSARY

Three Harlequin Reader Service 1995 shipments will contain respectively, coupons for entry into three different prize drawings, one for a Panasonic 31" wide-screen TV, another for a 5-piece Wedgwood china service for eight and the third for a Sharp ViewCam camcorder. To enter any drawing using an Entry Coupon, simply complete and mail according to directions.

There is no obligation to continue using the Reader Service to enter and be eligible for any prize drawing. You may also enter any drawing by hand printing the words "Prize Surprise," your name and address on a 3"x5" card and the name of the prize you wish that entry to be considered for (i.e., Panasonic wide-screen TV, Wedgwood china or Sharp ViewCam). Send your 3"x5" entries via first-class mail (limit: one per envelope) to: Prize Surprise Sweepstakes 3448, c/o the prize you wish that entry to be considered for, P.O. Box 1315, Buffalo, NY 14269-1315, USA or P.O. Box 610, Fort Erie, Ontario L2A 5X3, Canada.

To be eligible for the Panasonic wide-screen TV, entries must be received by 6/30/95; for the Wedgwood china, 8/30/95; and for the Sharp ViewCam, 10/30/95.

Winners will be determined in random drawings conducted under the supervision of D.L. Blair, Inc., an independent judging organization whose decisions are final, from among all eligible entries received for that drawing. Approximate prize values are as follows: Panasonic wide-screen TV ($1,800); Wedgwood china ($840) and Sharp ViewCam ($2,000). Sweepstakes open to residents of the U.S. (except Puerto Rico) and Canada, 18 years of age or older. Employees and immediate family members of Harlequin Enterprises, Ltd., D.L. Blair, Inc., their affiliates, subsidiaries and all other agencies, entities and persons connected with the use, marketing or conduct of this sweepstakes are not eligible. Odds of winning a prize are dependent upon the number of eligible entries received for that drawing. Prize drawing and winner notification for each drawing will occur no later than 15 days after deadline for entry eligibility for that drawing. Limit: one prize to an individual, family or organization. All applicable laws and regulations apply. Sweepstakes offer void wherever prohibited by law. Any litigation within the province of Quebec respecting the conduct and awarding of the prizes in this sweepstakes must be submitted to the Regies des loteries et Courses du Quebec. In order to win a prize, residents of Canada will be required to correctly answer a time-limited arithmetical skill-testing question. Value of prizes are in U.S. currency.

Winners will be obligated to sign and return an Affidavit of Eligibility within 30 days of notification. In the event of noncompliance within this time period, prize may not be awarded. If any prize or prize notification is returned as undeliverable, that prize will not be awarded. By acceptance of a prize, winner consents to use of his/her name, photograph or other likeness for purposes of advertising, trade and promotion on behalf of Harlequin Enterprises, Ltd., without further compensation, unless prohibited by law.

For the names of prizewinners (available after 12/31/95), send a self-addressed, stamped envelope to: Prize Surprise Sweepstakes 3448 Winners, P.O. Box 4200, Blair, NE 68009.

RPZ KAL